Murder in a Manner of Speaking

Elaine Astolat, a shy and retiring young novelist, is persuaded to embark upon a new career as a speaker to literary societies and luncheon clubs when she becomes a client of the Crispin Speakers' Agency, whose office is in a quiet old riverside warehouse on the edge of London's redeveloped dockland. But Astolat soon discovers that even in the innocent milieu of literary societies there may lurk a thoroughly poisonous serpent. Passion is not far below the surface, people are not what they seem, and before long she finds herself caught in a spider's web of deception and murder, in a manner of speaking.

Readers of Hazel Wynn Jones's first novel, *Death and the Trumpets of Tuscany*, can look forward to a similar blend of entertainment and excitement as she draws an amused but affectionate picture of literary societies and luncheon clubs, a world where she is clearly very much at home.

CHAPTER 1

GETTING TO KNOW YOU

'Lucinda,' I cried, 'I am a patient woman, but this time you have gone too far! You are nothing but a sexy little slagbag, and I am going to *kill* you!'

Ta-ta-ta-ta-ta! That was the end of Lucinda, with her tawny hair and her eyes that gleamed with emerald depths when they weren't looking like chips of green ice. Lucinda had been wiped out by a line of little black crosses.

Zzipp! I whipped the paper out of the typewriter, screwed it up and threw it into the wastepaper basket.

As Elaine Astolat, the novelist, I am a force to be reckoned with. I make my characters do what I want, and if they fail to please me, I destroy them ruthlessly, as I had just destroyed Lucinda. I know my job. My books sell well, and they disappear off the shelves of public libraries like snow in summer. To paraphrase Hilaire Belloc, my prose is purple, but my books are read.

Life, alas, is not nearly as satisfactory as a novel. In real life I'm totally lacking in self-confidence, afraid to query the milk bill, shy as a young fawn. In my novels, shy fawns end up blissfully in the arms of tall, strong, handsome men. In real life, as I know only too well, shy fawns get shoved to the back of the queue and left there.

And 'shy as a fawn' sounds ridiculous when applied to a young woman with a string of successful books to her pseudonym. (You didn't think I was born with the name Elaine Astolat, did you? No, of course you didn't. You recognized it at once as an allusion to one of Tennyson's barmier heroines. But the name looks well on dust jackets, and it provides me with a convenient mask to hide behind.)

Success brings its problems, and it had brought me a beauty—an invitation to join the glittering throng of famous people who belong to the Crispin Speakers' Agency and who trip merrily round the country, talking about themselves to clubs and literary societies and getting paid for doing so. (I used to belong to a literary society myself once. We met every month to hear lectures by speakers of all kinds. It never occurred to me to wonder how the secretary of the society found all those speakers. Now I realized that he simply booked them through an organization like the Crispin Speakers' Agency.)

I was flattered at the idea of mixing with these people, and at the very least, I told myself, some of them would provide me with material for future novels. And so, in a moment of weakness, I swallowed the bait.

Now I was feeling the hook. At midday I was due to attend a 'Getting to Know You' reception at the Royal Casterbridge Hotel to meet 'the bookers', the Presidents and Secretaries who would decide whether or not the members of their various clubs and societies would have the pleasure of my company in the coming year.

My first instinct was to run away and hide—overlook the date—visit my dentist—anything. But Philippa Preston, the Agency's secretary, had purred over the phone that if the bookers didn't meet me, they wouldn't book me. (My own feeling was that if they *did* meet me they probably wouldn't book me either, because my natural shyness means that I don't shine in company.) On the other hand, I'd paid quite a lot of money for my ticket to attend the reception, and I decided to get my money's worth out of the Agency even if it killed me. Later on I was to recall that foolish phrase with a certain grim amusement.

I threw the cover over my typewriter and prepared to meet the dreaded bookers. Probably a rather conservative lot, I thought, and put on a plain suit of coffee-coloured silk and matching gloves, hoping to get by in the crowd.

It was a typical spring morning and pouring with rain, so I took a minicab to Mayfair, determined to arrive at the Royal Casterbridge in style. The doorman held his umbrella over me as I hurried up the steps into the foyer and made what I hoped was a grand entrance. The receptionist looked at me with cool disdain. The Crispin Speakers' Agency was 'Getting to Know You' in the Ballroom—and I was not going to be allowed to walk through the hotel corridor to get to it.

I crept down the steps again, out into the rain, along the side of the hotel and ducked into the entrance marked 'Ballroom.'

I walked down a slope of pale green carpet spattered with darker green rain-splashes. Crystal drops quivered in chandeliers above my head and were reflected in the peach-coloured mirrors along the walls. At the foot of the slope, a girl stood behind a table handing out round white name-badges to a group of loudly chattering, loudly dressed women. I wondered whether they were speakers or bookers. I hung back until they had departed, and then approached the girl.

'Elaine Astolat?' she said, and smiling brightly she ticked my name off her list. Then she looked at the badges laid out neatly on the table in front of her. She searched among the A's, and then among the E's. She looked at all the badges. She looked on the floor.

'Terribly sorry,' she said. 'Your badge doesn't seem to be here. Never mind, I'll write one for you.'

She scribbled something illegible on a plain white disc and pinned it on to my lapel.

'You'll find the Ladies' Room just round the corner,' she said, and waved me onward.

I opened the door and walked into the Ladies' Room. It sounded like the mynah house at the Zoo, and it was filled with creatures just as brightly coloured and just as noisy, squirting quantities of hairspray and perfume in all directions and giving glad cries of welcome to each other. It was like being a new girl at school again, and I did what most new girls do. I slipped into one of the loos and bolted the door.

Gradually the noise died down as the mynah birds departed in search of the bar, and I crept out of my hiding-place and looked at myself in the mirror. Small and slight, with straight dark hair cut in a 'twenties bob, I looked deplorably dull compared with the vivid mynah birds, and the white name-badge was quite useless as a means of identification—even *I* couldn't read my name on it. Still, I consoled myself with the thought that Philippa, the Agency secretary, would introduce me to some of the bookers. I followed the sound of the mynah birds and found the bar. With a glass in my hand I felt more courageous and moved into the Ballroom.

More chandeliers dripping crystal teardrops high above my head, more peach-coloured mirrors. A barrage of sound as several hundred people milled about, chattering and laughing and shrieking merrily at each other. The mirrored walls showed everybody having a wonderful time, except for one young woman in a coffee-coloured suit at the edge of the crowd. Me, of course.

It was the sort of situation in which I often place the heroine of a novel. She looks across the crowded room, she sees a handsome stranger, and almost at once their eyes meet in a long, long look . . . But I would have more sense than to place my heroine among a crowd of crumblies—there didn't seem to be anybody in the Ballroom under fifty, and not a spark of romance in the whole lot of them.

Gradually the crowd sorted itself out for me. I now saw that the mynah birds were scurrying about introducing themselves to the more soberly dressed members of the crowd, and then passing on, circulating, wheeling, and all the time—smiling. These, then, were the speakers. The soberly dressed people were the bookers, and they tended to move about in pairs, greeting the mynah birds and making notes in the pink booklets in their hands, for all the world like buyers at a sale. And of course that is what they were. This was a cattle market, and the cattle were expected to sell themselves.

Well, I did my best. I pinned a brave smile on my face (my heroines often do this in moments of adversity) and introduced myself boldly to complete strangers. They glanced at my badge, smiled politely and moved away. With all the row going on they probably couldn't hear me say my name—and they certainly couldn't read it on my badge. I cursed the girl who had scribbled it so carelessly, and I cursed my own cowardice in not asking for a clearly written badge.

The glass in my hand seemed to have emptied itself. I was about to return to the bar for a refill when an idea struck me. I would go back to the entrance and demand a fresh badge with my name clearly inscribed.

I turned and headed for the entrance. The girl had her back to me, and she was pinning a name-badge on to a tall, fair-haired man in a light tropical suit. He was bending down slightly towards her, and as he straightened up he looked past her and his eyes met mine in a long, long look . . .

I don't know how long we stood gazing at each other.

Then he smiled, a lovely, lazy smile, and said, 'Hi, Philippa!'

Philippa?

A middle-aged woman with frizzy yellow hair and a bright yellow dress stepped out from behind me and hurried towards him with outstretched hands. Philippa Preston, secretary to the Crispin Speakers' Agency, the woman I had been relying on to introduce me to the bookers.

'Darling!' she cried. 'Where have you been? Julian's getting quite worried about you . . .'

'Sorry I'm late, Philippa,' he said. 'The plane was

delayed. I've come straight from Heathrow. Can I leave my bag with you?'

He picked up his overnight bag and swung it over the table as he moved away with Philippa. It was an ordinary bag, a well-travelled bag, a badly scuffed bag. Nothing very interesting about it, except that I could just make out his name on the luggage-tag. Darius Underwood. A splendid name. I wondered if he pronounced it the old-fashioned way as Da-RY-us or the modern way as DA-rius, as in Milhaud.

I was still thinking about that when I noticed that his bag had caught one of the white badges on the table and had knocked it on to the floor. Quickly I scooped it up and darted away.

The Ladies' Room was empty now and pleasantly peaceful. I fished a pen out of my bag and wrote ASTOLAT in big black letters. My first badge had been a small disc, but this one was larger, and it was rectangular in shape. It looked quite handsome. I pinned it on and looked at myself in the mirror. ASTOLAT stood out boldly, which was a good thing. If there was one thing I had learned from watching the crowd, it was that most of the bookers needed reading glasses but would die rather than be seen wearing them.

The door opened suddenly and a small, elderly lady hurried in and collapsed into one of the armchairs. She was pale and breathless, fumbling in her handbag and gasping for air. I hurried over to her.

'Can I help you?' I asked. 'A glass of water?'

She nodded, and I fetched some water. She brought out a small gold pill-box, and with trembling hands took out a bright red pill.

'Red for danger,' she quavered, and smiled at me shakily.

I held the glass for her. She swallowed the pill, took a sip of water and then rested her head back against the chair, her eyes closed. Gradually the trembling ceased and her breathing became more normal.

'Thank you so much,' she said. 'Very kind . . . very kind
. . . but you mustn't let me keep you . . .'

I hesitated. Much as I wanted to go back to the Ballroom
and get to work on the bookers, I didn't like to leave the
old lady.

'There's no hurry,' I said. 'Stay here and rest for a bit
until you're feeling better. I expect it was the heat . . .'

She smiled and patted her white hair. 'It really is very
hot in there,' she said. 'And such a lot of people. I come
every year, and of course it's always a bit of a crush, but
this year seems worse than ever . . .'

(Or is it just that you are one year older, I thought.)

'But then lots of things about the Agency are not as nice
as they used to be. Do you find that?'

'I'm afraid I'm new here,' I said. 'This is my first visit.'

'Ah, then perhaps it's different for you. But I'm one of
the Agency's oldest bookers—' she gave a little giggle—'I
mean, I was one of their *very first* bookers. You see, I knew
Mary and Julian long before they set up the Agency . . .'

Vaguely I remembered seeing the names of Julian and
Mary on the Agency's headed notepaper.

'Julian Leigh and Mary Michaelmas, you know. They
were the stars of our local repertory theatre—that was the
old Theatre Royal at Bettesham—oh, many years ago.
Nowadays people say that Mary looks like the Queen
Mother—and I suppose in a way she does, because she's
very charming and she has a lovely smile, and of course I
have to remember that Mary must be well over sixty now
—but *I* can remember her playing Juliet . . .'

A faraway and very sweet smile appeared on her face. I
recalled seeing exactly the same expression on my grandmother's face when we'd been watching Peggy Ashcroft
playing some old woman on television. And my grandmother had said softly, 'I can remember Peggy Ashcroft
playing Juliet . . .' It's extraordinary how vividly people
remember actors and actresses from their young days.

'. . . I wrote to Mary about—about the way the Agency seems to be going downhill. I couldn't put it all in writing, of course, because you see I'm not *sure* . . . but I said I'd tell her all about it today. That's what's made me so nervous and silly, I expect . . . I'm so worried . . . you see, I don't want to hurt Mary's feelings . . . but then, if I don't speak out . . . well, it's not fair to leave her in ignorance of the nasty things that are going on—at least, I *think* they are going on . . . you do see, don't you, how difficult it all is? "I must be cruel only to be kind . . ." Dear me, I remember Julian saying that as Hamlet all those years ago . . . what a beautiful young man he was . . . but I do hate having to be cruel . . . especially to Mary . . . she's a perfect darling . . . but then if I keep quiet it may be so much worse for her in the long run . . .'

Her voice faltered and died away. I put down the glass of water and held her hand in mind. Her pulse seemed to be quite steady. We sat quietly together.

She wore an elegant but rather old-fashioned suit of soft blue wool, the colour of harebells, over a blouse of Brussels lace fastened high at her throat with a cameo of the Three Graces. A plain old-fashioned wedding ring, and on her right hand a big opal ring set with diamonds. Her handbag and shoes of lizard had been well cared for. She was what my grandmother would have immediately recognized as A Lady, and—after one look at the shoes and handbag— would have qualified as A Lady In Slightly Reduced Circumstances.

The old lady began to talk again. Her voice was stronger now.

'I'm afraid nothing is as nice nowadays . . . do you know, even my pot-pourri doesn't smell as nice as it used to . . .'

(My grandmother says the same thing. She also says that everybody mumbles nowadays.)

'Well, my dear, I mustn't keep you—I expect you want to get back to the reception and meet some of the speakers . . .'

Meet the *speakers*? I glanced at myself in the mirror. My sober appearance must have misled the old lady into thinking I was a booker like herself. Well, it didn't matter. I couldn't possibly try to sell myself to *her*.

'Tell me about Julian and Mary,' I said.

She smiled.

'It was all really rather romantic,' she said. 'Mary's father and mother came from old theatrical families and they brought her up to be a proper child of the theatre—she could paint a set or light a scene while she was still in her teens. But most of all, they taught her how to act. Her father was an actor-manager, and he ran the Bettesham Rep. I suppose in their early days he and his wife played the romantic leads, but by the time I knew them they were playing older parts, and Mary played the heroines . . .'

'When was this?' I asked.

'Oh . . . it must be forty years ago . . . Mary was only a little slip of a thing, but she was a first-class actress. But she needed somebody really good to play opposite her, and somehow they never seemed to be able to find the right man. And then out of the blue—Julian Leigh appeared. My dear, he was *sensational*! Well, I mean, he only played a few small parts at first, but you could see that he would be going on to higher things, and very soon he was playing opposite Mary . . .'

'Was he a good actor?' I asked.

'No, I suppose actually he wasn't a very good actor—but he looked so handsome, and his voice was so beautiful— and besides he was obviously head over heels in love with Mary, and she with him—it was always quite a thrill going to the theatre just to see them together . . .'

Her voice faded. She was looking back forty years.

'And then they did *Romeo and Juliet*, and on the opening night, after they'd taken their curtain calls, Mary's father —he was playing Old Capulet—he stepped forward and announced that Julian and Mary were getting married. Well, my dear, the audience went quite mad with delight. We were all so happy for them . . .'

Her voice tailed away again. I waited quietly.

'I heard afterwards that Mary's father made the same announcement after every performance . . . I suppose it was good for business, and I'm sure it was good theatre, and that would certainly have appealed to him . . . And so Mary and Julian got married. And the next week they played Beatrice and Benedick—Julian got a lot of laughs—all those lines where he has to say he'll never marry, you know . . .'

She smiled, and I smiled back.

'Oh yes, and then they did *The Importance of Being Earnest*, Mary played Gwendolen and her mother played Lady Bracknell—she's Gwendolen's mother, you know—and really she was quite formidable. "Inspired casting," the newspaper critic called it . . . And what a laugh Julian got with his line about all women becoming like their mothers . . . Oh yes, inspired casting . . .'

The door crashed open and a woman of imposing build charged in. Head poking forward and a dowager's hump. Brassy hair, a hard black pencil line where her eyebrows should have been, and unbelievably white teeth. On her head she had a velvet cocktail hat like a horrified hedgehog. It was decorated with a mass of quills sticking up like— well, like quills upon the fretful porcupine, as Shakespeare puts it. She stared around the room imperiously, and saw me.

'Where's Mrs Beresford?' she barked.

Then she caught sight of the old lady and moved towards her.

'Oh, Bunty, there you are!' she said. 'Whatever's the matter? You're not ill, are you?'

My little old lady looked up. She lifted her chin, and her faded blue eyes flashed.

'I am *not* ill, Verena,' she said firmly. 'I'm just having a nice little chat with this young lady . . .'

Verena glanced at me disdainfully. She obviously took me for a cloakroom attendant, and she did not have nice little chats with such people.

I turned away with the glass of water and busied myself emptying it into the basin and then drying it on some of the minute multi-coloured tissues thoughtfully issued by the management. As I did so, I mused upon Shakespeare's use of the strange word 'porpentine' when he so clearly meant 'porcupine'. After all, 'quills upon the fretful porcupine' conveys a much clearer picture of the animal in question with its prickles up, it sounds just as good and it scans just as well. Was it a simple spelling mistake on his part, or was it the fault of the printers? That seemed more likely. I've suffered quite a lot at the hands of printers—my prize to date going to the printer who transformed Miss Elaine Astolat into Miss Elastoplast, as though I was the winner of a rather unusual beauty contest.

At this point my thoughts were interrupted by a sharp 'clink'. The Porpentine had dropped a small—a very small —coin into the attendant's saucer.

'Now, Bunty, have you taken your pill?' she asked.

Bunty nodded.

'Well, for heaven's sake, come on! Mary's been asking for you . . . you said you wanted to talk to her, and you know how busy she is . . .'

She hustled Bunty away.

I was about to follow them (despite the fact that the Porpentine had allowed the door to swing shut in my face) when I noticed a small pink booklet lying on the chair. Bunty Beresford must have dropped it in her confusion. I picked it up, thinking to run after her and return it, when I noticed a message written in very large letters across the cover:

DO NOT ALLOW THIS BOOK TO BE READ BY ANY OF OUR SPEAKERS

Well, what would you have done?

I returned to the privacy of the loo, sat down and began to read.

CHAPTER 2

FALSE COLOURS

The book was a catalogue of the speakers and the subjects that they offered. It all seemed absolutely harmless, and I wondered why speakers were not allowed to read it.

The names were listed in alphabetical order, so mine came early on in the list, and I was agreeably surprised to find that they had spelled my name correctly. There were two numbers against my name which didn't seem to mean anything. I turned the pages quickly—Darius Underwood was on the last page, and the same two numbers appeared against his name. So we had something in common. It seemed a good omen.

UNDERWOOD, Darius. Author of several travel books. Spent one year in Turkey (*Anatolian Notebook*), two years in India (*Karachi Notebook*) and another in Marrakech (*Modern Marrakech: A Notebook*).

That explained the tropical suit, and the remark about coming straight from the airport, but the titles of the books did not look very promising.

I flicked idly through the pages. There was Charlie Spink, the Perky Pensioner, a lovable Cockney character who offered to tell Senior Citizens how to augment their income and get more fun out of life. The number against his name was twice as high as mine. I suddenly realized that the numbers represented a speaker's fees.

I read on.

Most people's fees were twice as high as mine. Some TV personalities asked three times as much.

No wonder the book was not supposed to fall into the hands of any of the speakers! I raged at the thought of the fees these people were getting compared with me. Then it occurred to me that if I sat there much longer I wasn't going to get any fees at all. I slipped the booklet into my handbag and returned to the fray.

How right I had been to write my name clearly on my new badge! It made all the difference in the world. Instead of my having to introduce myself to people, they came up and introduced themselves to me. Even the TV personalities smiled graciously upon me. I circulated. I began to enjoy the heady sensation of being a social success.

I caught sight of Darius Underwood and moved towards him, but my way was blocked by a dreadful little old man with an aluminium walking-stick. He had decorated the stick with a bunch of scarlet ribbons, and he pranced around me, grinning and passing the stick across his extended left arm as though he was playing a violin. He must be Charlie Spink, the Perky Pensioner. If that was the way he proposed that his fellow-pensioners should augment their incomes, I didn't give much for their chances.

There was a flash of yellow, and Philippa Preston went by, towing two elderly bookers in the direction of one of the TV personalities. I began moving in the direction of Darius Underwood.

The Fretful Porpentine charged across my path.

'Contessa!' she cried. 'Contessa!'

One of the mynah birds paused in mid-flight, and turned towards her. She was a plump, pretty little woman wearing a dress that was far too young for her. I recognized her at once. The Contessa della Stola was a romantic novelist whose name was as false as my own, and I had little doubt that her title of Contessa was self-bestowed. She advanced towards the Porpentine with every appearance of enthusiasm, embraced her and kissed her on both cheeks. The Porpentine glowed with pleasure. What a silly snob she was.

By this time Darius was surrounded by a number of elderly bookers. I decided to bide my time until I could get him to myself, and looked around for Bunty Beresford. She was talking to another little old lady who was dressed in lavender silk.

The lavender lady turned in my direction, and I saw a pair of laughing blue eyes and a mass of tight silvery curls that gave her the look of a merry little Dresden shepherdess. Her dress of lavender silk had silver threads running through it, and at her throat she wore a frothy jabot of silver lace. As she moved her hand I caught a flash of a magnificent amethyst ring. She must be Mary Michaelmas, Bunty's friend, the girl who had played Juliet all those years ago and who was now one of the owners of the Crispin Speakers' Agency. 'People say she looks like the Queen Mother,' Bunty had said. And so she did.

Where, I wondered, was her husband? My eye was caught once more by the yellow hair and yellow dress of Philippa Preston. She was leading a couple of women through the crush towards a tall, elderly man with a beautiful actor's face and a stunning mane of chestnut hair. This could only be Julian Leigh, the young man ('not a very good actor, but so handsome') who had married the only daughter of the theatre manager. To Bunty he had seemed a romantic figure. To me he sounded like a young man on the make. And he had done well for himself. Here he was, forty years on, the guiding spirit of the Crispin Speakers' Agency, wearing a suit of impeccable cut that murmured Savile Row. I doubted if Julian Leigh could have afforded such an expensive outfit when he was starring at the Bettesham Rep.

As Philippa approached with the two women, Julian's face lit up and he strode through the crowd towards them, his hands outstretched in a theatrical gesture of welcome. All the same, I didn't feel that he was really interested in them, except as a matter of business. Perhaps they were bookers for a well-to-do club which could afford to engage some of the expensive TV personalities (at three times my fee—that still rankled!).

His wife, on the other hand, was genuinely interested in her old friend Bunty, and her pretty little face was troubled. As I watched, Mary leaned towards Bunty and patted her hand as though to reassure her—a gesture that reminded me of the way my grandmother used to comfort me when I poured out my troubles to her. I noticed that in comparison with Mary's amethyst ring, Bunty's beautiful opal looked like a pinhead, and that to me meant only one thing— Mary's amethyst was as phoney as the colour of her husband's hair.

Then some mynah birds flocked around me, and after a brief conversation with them I resumed my attempt to reach Darius Underwood. Once more I was thwarted, this time by the sound of a large bell ringing and Philippa Preston calling for quiet.

I looked around. Julian Leigh had ditched the two women and was standing at the far end of the Ballroom, looking like Mark Antony about to address the mob.

'Ladies and gentlemen,' he said, '*delightful* to have you all here again.' (Bunty was right—he had a beautiful voice.) 'Now we come to the stage in the proceedings when some of our speakers come to the microphone and have just two minutes to tell you about themselves, and to give you a taste of the talks that they offer for your members. May I ask you to find yourself seats, and then I will call upon our first speaker.'

Waiters appeared with little gilt chairs, and we all scattered and found seats for ourselves. I tried to get a seat near

Darius, but ended up sitting next to the Fretful Porpentine, with Bunty and Mary on her other side. My left-hand neighbour was a woman in a cerise dress. She smiled at me and looked at my badge.

'What a pretty name that is,' she said. 'Where is Astolat?'

That floored me.

'*Who* is Astolat?' That I could have understood. But— '*Where* is Astolat?' Perhaps she was making a covert allusion to Tennyson's *Idylls* . . .

I smiled.

'It's—er—it's on the way to Camelot,' I said, and waited for her response.

Her face was blank.

'Oh, how *interesting*,' she said, lying in her teeth, and turned to speak to her other neighbour.

And then, for the first time, I noticed that there were two different kinds of badges: a small round one, which signified that the wearer was a speaker, and a large rectangular one which betokened a booker. *And I was wearing a large rectangular badge!*

No wonder all the mynah birds had been so nice to me. No wonder the TV personalities had smiled upon me. I was an impostor! Any minute now that dreadful Philippa woman would tear off my badge and demote me to the ranks of the speakers. Guiltily, and feeling sure that everybody was watching me, I tried to remove the badge, but to no avail. I sank lower and lower on my little gilt chair. I was so wrapped up in my embarrassment that the first speaker came and went without making any impression on me. There was a patter of applause.

The next speaker walked to the microphone. She was an elderly woman dressed in rather dowdy clothes and sensible shoes, and she turned out to be a writer of very good historical novels. She was not much of a speaker, but she certainly knew her subject. She explained how she worked out her stories, how she did her research, and how she worked every day from nine to five. Her three key-words, she said, were Imagination, Verification and Organization. This was exactly how I proposed to give my talk, if anybody ever booked me.

I applauded vigorously. To my surprise, the rest of the applause was lukewarm.

'Poison!' hissed the Fretful Porpentine in my right ear.

I stared at her in astonishment.

'Poison?' I asked.

'All that talk about how she goes about her work—makes it sound as dull as working for the Gas Board,' said the Porpentine. 'My members aren't going to pay to hear that sort of rubbish. They like *reading* books, but they don't want to know how they're made. It's like going into the supermarket for a can of beans—you just take a can off the shelf, and that's it. You don't want to know how the beans got into the can.'

I gulped. I had never taken a particularly elevated view of my work, but I had certainly never thought of it as being akin to stuffing beans into a can. Clearly I should have to revise my ideas before I addressed the literary societies and luncheon clubs of England—if I ever did . . .

I tried once more to unpin the badge, and once more I failed. I was so deep in this that I also failed to register that Julian was introducing Darius Underwood as the next speaker.

'And *yes*, he pronounces his name DA-rius, to rhyme with Marius,' said Julian, and with a graceful gesture he waved Darius towards the microphone, and Darius strode through the crumblies on their little gilt chairs like a visitor from another world.

'Ladies and gentlemen,' he began. He had a pleasant voice and an easy, confident manner, and I looked forward to an enjoyable two minutes.

There was a sudden commotion on the far side of the Fretful Porpentine, who jumped to her feet with a loud cry.

Bunty Beresford had collapsed.

She was slumped gasping in her chair. Mary Michaelmas was trying to hold her up, patting her hand and murmuring words of encouragement.

Darius left the microphone and moved swiftly towards the little group. He swept Bunty up in his arms like a baby.

Philippa Preston hurried forward and cleared a path for him to carry Bunty out of the room. Mary and the Porpentine followed, looking anxious.

Everyone began talking at once, until Julian called us all to order.

'I'm afraid Mrs Beresford has been taken ill . . . *please* don't worry . . . nothing *serious* . . . everything is being taken care of . . . Philippa is looking after her . . . *no* cause for alarm . . .'

And then Darius returned. He strode up to the microphone and cut short Julian's reassuring waffle.

'Is there a doctor here? We need help immediately . . .'

My neighbour in the cerise dress got up and went towards him. Together they hurried in the direction of the Ladies' Room.

Once more Julian took centre stage. He dominated the whole room, and his voice rode easily above our chattering.

'Quiet, please!' he said. '*Quiet*, please!'

And we were quiet.

'Our next speaker,' said Julian, 'is a *very* old friend—he really needs no introduction from me—Charlie Spink, the Perky Pensioner!'

Charlie Spink homed in on the microphone, cheerily waved his be-ribboned walking-stick and began to sing a lovable Cockney song. That I could *not* stand. I stood up and pushed my way through the crowd.

I saw Darius standing on guard outside the door of the Ladies' Room. He opened the door for me and I went in.

Mary was seated on a low couch, holding a limp, pale-faced Bunty in her arms. The doctor in the cerise dress was kneeling at her feet, while Philippa and the Porpentine stood in the background looking down helplessly.

Nobody took any notice of me. I didn't quite know why I was there. I felt that there was something important I ought to tell the doctor, but I couldn't remember what it was.

I looked at the cerise dress, and the phrase 'red for danger' floated through my mind.

The doctor stood up slowly, and I knew that it was too late for whatever it was that I had to say.

Bunty Beresford was dead.

Well, at least she died in the arms of her old friend. I should not have liked to think of her dying with only the Porpentine to comfort her.

There didn't seem to be anything that I could do, so I slipped out quietly and made my way home. For the whole of the rest of the day I mourned for Bunty. I took it for granted that she had died from natural causes. It didn't occur to me that I had witnessed murder, in a manner of speaking.

CHAPTER 3

CRISPIN WHARF HOUSE

The rains of spring were followed by the rains of summer. I stayed firmly indoors, finished writing one novel and started writing another, and had forgotten the Crispin Speakers' Agency (or had pushed it to the back of my mind) when one morning in July I received my first booking form. A Ladies' Luncheon Club in Hertfordshire wanted me to visit them in November to talk about *Romantic Novelists Today*. I noted the date in my diary, sent off an acceptance form (pink) to the Club Secretary, a confirmation form (yellow) to the Agency, and got on with my new novel. It was going to be my best ever.

Three months later, when I was glancing through my diary in October, I realized what I had let myself in for, and then I panicked. I grabbed the phone and babbled incoherently to the person the other end. Luckily it was Philippa Preston, the imperturbable organizer of the 'Getting to Know You' reception at the Royal Casterbridge.

'—and the Fretful Porpentine said her members didn't want to know how baked beans were stuffed into cans,' I wailed.

Philippa didn't waste time trying to sort that one out.

'Come over to the office right away,' she said. 'It's easy to find us. We're in Rotherhithe—Crispin Wharf House, end of Crispin Wharf Street. Just head for the river . . .'

And throw myself in, I thought gloomily.

It was a pleasant sunny afternoon. I took the bus to Rotherhithe. An elderly woman got off the bus with me.

'Excuse me,' I said. 'Could you tell me the way to Crispin Wharf Street?'

She dumped her heavy shopping-bag on the pavement and looked at me.

'You don't want to go to Crispin Wharf Street, dearie,' she said. 'There's nothing there. All bombed to bits it was, forty years ago . . . My mum and dad was living there then, and they was bombed out . . . terrible mess the place was . . . no, you don't want to go to Crispin Wharf Street.'

'But I'm looking for Crispin Wharf House,' I said. 'It's in Crispin Wharf Street, by the river.'

'I don't know, I'm sure,' she said doubtfully. 'But then I've not been down there since the Blitz, and that's a fact. Still, if you're sure you want Crispin Wharf Street, you just follow the main road here until you come to the big dry-cleaners on the corner, turn right, and you'll be in Crispin Wharf Street.'

'Thanks very much,' I said.

'Or you could take the short cut down Magpie Lane,' she said. 'That runs down by the river and comes out at the bottom of Crispin Wharf Street.'

'Where is Magpie Lane?' I asked.

'See that black and white pub acrost the road?' she said. 'That's the Magpie. The lane runs alongside it . . .'

'Many thanks,' I said. 'I'll try Magpie Lane . . .'

The Magpie Inn was an ancient building of black beams and white plaster, with a weathercock in the shape of a magpie perched high above the crazy old tiled roof. It looked as though it had survived not only the Blitz but also the Great Fire of London. Beyond the Inn a narrow lane wound between grim, grey buildings the colour of long-dead embers. Gaunt iron walkways overhead threw criss-cross shadows across the lane. The whole place had a seedy, slightly sinister air, that sent a chill through me. Two heavy posts, joined by an iron bar, stood sentry across the mouth of the lane to keep out everything except foot traffic. I got the message: Keep Out. This Means You. I decided to take the main road and go the long way round.

The main road was dull—just a succession of shops and flats and offices, and a lot of fast-moving traffic. But at last I reached the corner with the drycleaners, turned right, and started to walk down Crispin Wharf Street.

It was a sad place—on the right-hand side some derelict buildings with their windows boarded up, on the left a large open space surrounded by high chain-link fencing. I wondered where the elderly lady's parents had lived. At the far end of the street, backing on to the river, stood a squat, grey brick building with iron bars at the windows like a prison. It seemed an odd place for the headquarters of the glamorous Crispin Speakers' Agency.

To the left there was a walled builder's yard, open to the sky, and between the two buildings hung a curtain of leafy green and yellow creepers.

A narrow lane twisted away to the right, a dark canyon flanked by tall grey buildings as forbidding as mediæval fortresses. A notice high up on one wall told me that this was the other end of Magpie Lane. An old black bollard set in the mouth of the lane repeated the message of the bar and two posts at the other end: Keep Out. This Means You. I was glad I'd come round by the road, even though it had been a very long way round.

I hurried towards Crispin Wharf House, and when I was within a few yards of it I was conscious of a curious and utterly unexpected feature: there was a strong and very pleasant smell of spices. I sniffed the air: cloves, pepper, cinnamon, nutmeg—and did I detect a whiff of curry? It was a friendly, homely, welcoming smell, as incongruous as it was surprising. It was as though a surly-looking guard dog had wagged its tail and rolled over to be tickled. There were no shops in Crispin Wharf Street, so the smell had to be coming from the House itself. Could the Agency be dealing in spices as well as in speakers? The thought flashed through my mind and was forgotten as a woman with frizzy yellow hair came out and waved to me. Philippa Preston.

'Hi, Astolat!' she called. 'Come on in . . .'

To the right of Crispin Wharf House there was a short alley with honeysuckle sprouting from the wall, growing from cracks between the bricks wherever there was room for a root to lodge itself. Philippa was standing at the entrance to the alley. Behind her a little iron gate led to a small square landing-stage attached to the house. And beyond the landing-stage, the River Thames.

I had no time to look around. Philippa opened a green door in the side of Crispin Wharf House and ushered me inside.

After its forbidding grey exterior, the interior was a knock-out. The whole of the ground floor was one vast living area, with silver-grey ships' timbers supporting the ceiling, which was striped with more silver-grey beams. A white spiral staircase corkscrewed its way towards an upper floor. There were chairs and couches of pale Italian leather, a long table with a heavy glass top, and lamps wherever they might be needed. Floor-length wall-mirrors made the place look even larger than it was.

Two huge windows, shaped like old-fashioned baker's ovens, overlooked the river, and a pair of french windows led out on to the landing-stage, which an estate agent might describe as a deceptively spacious riverside patio, but which barely had room for a table and a couple of white canvas chairs.

The corner of the room by the french windows served as the Agency office, with a big desk for Philippa and comfortable chairs for her guests. There was a glorious smell of freshly roasted coffee coming from a percolator bubbling gently on a low table. I sank into a deep armchair and Philippa brought me a cup of coffee, took one herself, and settled down behind her desk. Through the french windows I could see a long black Tate and Lyle barge moving rapidly downstream, its dark red sails furled. It was all very different from my editor's office.

'Have you got a notebook with you?' asked Philippa.

Of course I had a notebook with me. A writer is never completely off duty.

'Now,' she said, 'how are you going to begin your talk?'

'I d-don't know,' I said, alarmed. 'I haven't thought . . .'

'OK,' said Philippa. 'Begin "Madam President, and ladies, it gives me great pleasure to come here today . . ." It's not much of a line, but it will get you started.'

I wrote it down in my notebook, and then looked up.

'Now,' she said, 'think of a good closing line. And if you can't think of anything original, use a bit of poetry in praise of love. What's that Shakespeare thing about the marriage of true minds?'

I tried to remember.

'"Love's rosy lips . . ." no . . . "Love alters not . . ." yes, yes, I've got it!

"Love's not Time's fool, though rosy lips and cheeks
Within his bending sickle's compass come.
Love alters not with his brief hours and weeks
But bears it out even to the edge of doom."'

'That's it!' said Philippa. 'That's how you bring your talk to a close.'

'But what about the meat in the sandwich?' I said.

'I'm afraid that's up to you,' she said. 'But if you're absolutely stuck, have one of your books with you and read a few passages from it. Oh, and learn your talk off by heart —*and* your readings. You only *pretend* to read—the audience wants to see your face, not the top of your head.'

'How did you learn all this?' I asked, when I had written it all down in my notebook.

'I haven't spent the best part of my life working for Julian and Mary without learning how they put on a performance,' she said.

'Have you known them a long time?' I asked.

'About thirty years,' said Philippa. 'Long before you were born . . . Julian and Mary were the stars at the Bettesham Repertory Theatre and I was assistant stage manager, assistant publicity officer and assistant-just-about-everything-else. Then the theatre folded—that must have been—ten . . . fifteen years ago . . . wait, I've got some photographs here—we're going to use them on the poster for their new show—it's to be a recital of poetry and prose on the subject of love—Julian's calling it *A Lover and his Lass* . . .'

She produced a folder of large, glossy photographs and laid them out before me on the desk. Julian and Mary as Romeo and Juliet. Julian and Mary as Hamlet and Ophelia. Julian and Mary as Elyot and Amanda. Mary as the Duchess of Malfi about to be murdered. Julian as Sydney

Carton about to do a far, far better thing. No Ayckbourn, no Beckett, no Osborne, no Pinter . . . I could well understand why Bettesham Rep closed. The surprising thing was that it had lasted so long.

'After the theatre closed,' said Philippa, 'Julian took me on as his secretary and we all moved in here. Old warehouses like this were going cheap in those days. Julian had all sorts of projects, but they didn't come off. He did some readings on radio, and a tremendous number of voice-overs—you know, commentaries for documentary films, or sales pitches for television commercials, not really his kind of thing. Mary did some television work—she's got her own afternoon chat show now, *Tea with Mary Michaelmas*—do you ever watch it?'

I shook my head.

'I'm always at work in the afternoon.'

'Try to catch it sometimes if you can,' said Philippa. 'You'd learn quite a lot about technique. So, as I was saying, Mary did some television work, and she did a few talks for luncheon clubs—and that's really how the Agency began. At first the only speakers on our books were Julian and Mary, but then they brought in a few old friends, and after a bit the whole thing snowballed, and—well, here we are.'

'I hadn't realized that this place used to be a warehouse,' I said. 'Was it by any chance used for storing spices? I noticed a lovely spicy smell when I arrived outside.'

Philippa laughed.

'We've been here so long we don't notice the smell any more,' she said.

'I suppose brick walls retain smell in the same way that they retain heat,' I said.

'I'd never thought of that,' she said. 'Perhaps they do. In that case, we're lucky that this place used to hold something as pleasant as spices. Would you like some more coffee?'

'Please,' I said.

'Now,' said Philippa, when she had refilled both our cups. 'Clothes. Have you got any romantic ones?'

I shook my head.

She looked at me and sighed. I was wearing a short holly-green coat and a red holly-berry scarf thrown hastily over my usual working outfit of sweater and jeans.

'You look very sweet,' she said. 'But—well—you *do* look a bit like a student applying for her first job. If you're going to be one of our speakers you have to be professional and dress for the part.'

I thought with horror of the mynah birds at the Royal Casterbridge reception—had *they* been dressed for the part? Did she expect me to look like *them*?

'Why do you think I wore that bright yellow dress at the Royal Casterbridge?' she asked. 'Not because it flattered my complexion! It was so that Julian and Mary could spot me quickly whenever they wanted me. I was professional. I dressed for the part.'

She was certainly dressed now for the part of the Agency's organizer. A severe tobacco-brown suit over a plain white blouse, spectacles on a gold chain around her neck—an efficient, no-nonsense dreadnought.

'Did you notice Mary Michaelmas at the reception, all lavender and lace?' she asked.

I nodded.

'When Mary's relaxing at home here she often wears an old track suit—but in public she always looks as pretty as a picture. *She dresses for the part.*'

'Yes, but—'

'Clothes are very important when you make public appearances,' said Philippa. 'Your readers will make up a good part of your audiences, and they'll expect you to look like their idea of a romantic novelist, all floaty and ethereal.'

I couldn't tell her that most romantic novelists don't look like that at all—at least, not the ones that I've met. Some of them are nice motherly women in sensible tweeds and twinsets; some are shy fawns like me; and quite a few are men. Not one of them could be described as floaty and ethereal.

'Mary gets most of her clothes from an old friend, Madame Bamba,' said Philippa. 'She runs a dress salon in Mayfair—Bambinetta. I'll give you an introduction to her.'

'Oh, but I couldn't afford Mayfair prices!' I said.

Philippa smiled.

'Bamba also runs Bamba's Dress Hire in a shop off the Charing Cross Road—I suspect that's where she started. If you can't afford to buy from Bambinetta, you can probably afford to hire from Bamba. I'll give you a card, and then she'll allow you a discount . . .'

She wrote, in her neat, precise handwriting:

Madame Bamba. This is to introduce my friend Elaine Astolat. Philippa Preston, Crispin Speakers' Agency.

'There you are,' she said, and handed the card to me.

I made a quick note to check if these things were tax-deductible, and as I looked up again I saw that Philippa was looking at my left hand. I caught her eye, and she flushed.

'I'm sorry,' she said. 'I was just looking to see if you were wearing a wedding ring.'

'Not any more,' I said shortly, and she dropped the subject.

'Before we invited you to become one of our speakers I read some of your books, to make sure that you were the right person for us. In *my* day, romance was Celia Johnson saying goodbye to Trevor Howard at a railway station, but things are very different nowadays. Tell me, how do you write your stories?'

'I look at people in the street, or on television,' I said. 'Or perhaps I see a face in a magazine. Then I say to myself, "What would happen if . . .?", and I sit down at my typewriter and write a story about them. It's quite easy, really—much easier than talking to people.'

Philippa smiled. 'You sound like the Lady of Shalott,' she said. 'Julian recorded it last week for Radio 3. She lived in a tower and wove pictures of people that she saw in a mirror. Was she any relation to Elaine of Astolat?'

'No,' I said. 'But now I think of it, they both ended up dying for love and drifting downstream in a barge.'

'Making a thorough nuisance of themselves and constituting a danger to shipping,' said Philippa drily.

I smiled to myself. Philippa was not the sort to sympathize with young women who died of unrequited love. But she had an uncomfortable knack of hitting nails smartly upon the head. She was right about me. I was imprisoned in a tower, just like the Lady of Shalott, but my tower was simply my own lack of self-confidence. That image stayed with me for a long time.

All the same, I was beginning to feel relaxed under the influence of Philippa's brisk common sense. I even felt brave enough to ask a very important question.

'You talked about dressing for the part,' I said. 'I seem to remember that at the Royal Casterbridge reception there was a man in a tropical suit—was *he* just dressed for the part?'

Philippa shot me a quick glance, but I had my mask on —I was a simple inquirer after knowledge. Not a young woman fishing for information about a young man. Oh no . . .

'Ah, that was Darius Underwood,' said Philippa, and at the mention of his name the simple inquirer's heart gave a little flip. 'No, he wasn't just dressed for the part—he really *had* come back from somewhere hot—I forget where he'd been—I know he came straight from the airport.'

Philippa hadn't noticed me standing at the name-badge table when Darius had arrived and she had swept him off. Why should she? My back had been towards her—and even if I'd been facing her she would hardly have noticed a mousy young woman in a coffee-coloured suit. (Let's face it, 'coffee-coloured' is dress manufacturer's jargon for 'mud-coloured'. It makes you wonder what kind of coffee they drink—certainly nothing like Philippa's glorious brew.)

'Darius is one of Mary's discoveries—she met him at the television studios and invited him to join the Agency—she said it was high time we got some younger people on our books.'

'Ah,' I said, as a little light dawned upon me. 'And is that why you invited me to join?'

Philippa was not in the least abashed.

'Let's say it was one of the reasons,' she said. 'Your reputation as a novelist was the main one—we think that your name will be a draw in itself.'

I purred.

'But yes, most of our authors are getting on, so we need some younger people. Darius isn't an experienced speaker, but he gets quite a few engagements—he's been to fairly exotic places, and that seems to appeal to the bookers. He'll have a couple of years to prove himself, and if, after that, he's not bringing in much income we shall regretfully have to drop him.'

I sensed a chilly little wind blowing through the room, and it didn't come from the river. Those speakers who were 'getting on' and failing to bring in a good income for the Agency—they too would be dropped from the books, even though they were the 'old friends' who'd been brought in at the very start of the Agency. There was no need to ask whose hand would administer the *coup de grâce*. I couldn't imagine Julian or Mary doing it—but Philippa wouldn't shed any sentimental tears over the breaking of old ties. She was quite right, of course. The Agency was a business, not a Darby and Joan club. All the same, I felt sorry for anybody who relied upon the Agency as a major source of income.

'And in the meantime,' she said, 'Darius is useful in other ways—Julian and Mary have bought themselves a boat,

and he's teaching them to handle it. Julian says the river is
the highway of the future.'

It sounded as though Julian had been doing some voice-
overs for the Tourist Board.

'Oh, good, here he comes,' she said, and my heart gave
another flip.

Darius? *Here? Now?*

Through the windows I could see a smart white cabin
cruiser approaching. There were red-and-white lifebelts flat
on the roof of the cabin, and white rope fenders like small
bolsters hanging over the sides. The boat came close to the
little landing-stage and waited while some unseen person
got off. I waited too.

The landing-stage was small and square, surrounded by
strong white safety railings. There was a deep weatherboard
across the bottom of the french windows, and I guessed that
there were times when the highway of the future could
become a little too high for comfort.

A head appeared at the top of the landing-stage's small
fixed ladder—a head topped with improbable chestnut hair.
Not Darius, but Julian Leigh.

My excitement disappeared.

The boat moved away again, and I craned my neck to
see if Darius was at the helm. But I could see nothing of
any interest, except perhaps the name painted on the hull
—the *Silver Swan*. Doubtless that was Julian's idea.

Julian climbed up on to the landing-stage. He looked
superb in navy blue blazer, white turtle-neck sweater and
white pants. But was it, I wondered, quite appropriate for
Rotherhithe?

Philippa hurried out on to the landing-stage to join him.

'Hi, Julian,' she said. 'We've got one of our new speakers
here—Elaine Astolat. You know, the romantic novelist . . .'

It was obvious that without Philippa's prompting Julian
would have had no idea who Elaine Astolat was, but he
picked up his cue immediately. He took a couple of steps

across the landing-stage and paused, so that he was framed
in the french windows with the sunlit River Thames as a
backdrop. Then he put on a warm smile and stepped
into the room (without so much as a glance down at the
weatherboard—he must have practised that entrance a
good many times to avoid tripping). He took a quick
sidelong look into the nearest wall-mirror, ruffled his hair
gracefully and then advanced towards me, both hands
outstretched.

'Elaine, the lily maid of Astolat!' he cried. 'Lovely, *lovely*
name . . .'

Of course I ought to have played up to him. I ought to
have fluttered prettily towards him and put both my hands
in his, but I couldn't do it. My new-found self-confidence
deserted me. I put my left hand firmly in my coat pocket,
stuck out my right hand, walked forward and shook his
hand.

It ruined his entrance and he was not pleased with me. I
was not very pleased with me either. I had behaved awkwardly and ungraciously, not at all the way a successful
novelist is expected to behave.

Philippa stepped into the room.

'Darius is just coming,' she said.

And there he was, climbing up the ladder and swinging
himself up on to the landing-stage. Tall, fair, blue-eyed, just
as I remembered him. He was wearing an old grey jersey
and grey pants, not as decorative as Julian's outfit but far
more practical.

He crossed the wooden landing-stage in three strides, and
then he was in the room.

My heart went into overdrive.

Philippa introduced us, and I saw that he didn't remember me at all from the Royal Casterbridge reception. Still,
he seemed pleased to meet me, and as we shook hands it
seemed to me that he held my hand a little longer than was
strictly necessary. We stood looking at each other.

'Philippa, darling, what are these *gruesome* objects doing here?'

Julian had pounced upon the Bettesham Repertory photographs.

'I thought they might be useful publicity pictures for *A Lover and his Lass*,' said Philippa.

'Ah yes,' said Julian. 'How are the bookings going?'

'We've got a good few already,' said Philippa. 'We shall have to have some big posters made. I thought you might like to select some of the Bettesham Rep pictures to surround the main pictures of you and Mary . . .'

'Bring them over here, darling,' said Julian. 'Let's have a look at them . . .'

Philippa took the photographs over to the glass-topped table and began to spread them out. Julian leaned over them, his back towards me. He was very clearly and firmly shutting me out. Elaine Astolat simply did not exist for him.

'I'd better be going,' I said awkwardly. 'Thanks for helping me, Philippa.'

'Do you have far to go?' asked Darius.

His voice was not as beautiful as Julian's, but it sounded deep and very pleasant.

'Only as far as the Magpie bus stop in the main road,' I said, preparing to run away and hide myself in the safety of the Lady of Shalott's tower.

'May I walk you there?' said Darius. 'It's on my way.'

I could feel Philippa watching me, wondering if I would rebuff Darius as I had just rebuffed Julian. Of course I wanted Darius to walk me to the bus stop—and yet there I was shrinking back, unsure of myself.

Darius smiled, a lovely, slow smile. Did he understand that I was hesitating out of shyness, not because I disliked him?

'It's on my way,' he said again.

'Thanks very much,' I said, and allowed him to lead me out of Crispin Wharf House.

Once outside, I was about to walk up the street past the derelict buildings when Darius laid his hand lightly on my left arm and indicated Magpie Lane.

'This is a short cut,' he said. 'And it's far more interesting than the main road.'

I drew back.

'Oh, it looks a bit . . . grim,' I said. 'It's like something out of Dickens.'

'Not when you get to know it,' said Darius. 'You can't always judge by appearances, can you?'

He smiled, and led me into Magpie Lane.

CHAPTER 4

MAGPIE LANE

An ancient black bollard was set firmly in the middle of the worn stone paving, closing the lane against cars. On either side of the lane massive grey warehouses lowered over me, their windows barred like dungeons. Those on the left, the river side, were linked to those on the right by iron gangways high above my head. The afternoon sunlight caught the crisscross patterns of the guard rails on the gangways and threw heavy black shadows across the lane. There was no street lighting. It was a forbidding place by day. It would be a terrifying place by night.

As we passed the first warehouse I noticed a date set high in the grey brick wall. I stopped and looked up at it. 1888.

'Wait a minute,' I said. 'Dickens died in 1870.'

'So?' said Darius.

'Just now I said these buildings looked like something out of Dickens, but I was wrong,' I said. 'They weren't put up until nearly twenty years after his death. They're only about a hundred years old.'

'Does it matter?' said Darius, smiling.

'No,' I said a little doubtfully. 'But I like to get my facts right. I might want to use them in a book some time.'

'Do you think your readers would care?' D asked.

'*I* care,' I said shortly.

We walked on in silence. I felt guilty. I hadn't meant to snap at him like that. I stole a sidelong look at him to see if he was angry. At that moment he was looking sidelong at me. Our eyes met, we laughed, and the awkward moment was over.

Magpie Lane was more interesting than I had expected. Some of the old grey warehouses had creepers hanging from small cranes, some had window-boxes full of flowers, and one even had a small buddleia sprouting from its roof. Some had big double doors like garages, while others had small side doors like the one at Crispin Wharf House. And nearly all of them had freshly painted signboards.

'So people are still working here?' I said, surprised.

'Indeed they are,' said Darius. 'Take a look . . .'

I read some of the names on the signboards: Andrews and Lawson, Rhodrons Research, Lillystone and Stephens, Ryeworth Press . . .'

'A lot of them are in computers,' said Darius. 'Don't ask me what they do, because I don't know. Ryeworth Press, as you can see, is a small printing firm. There are quite a few architects and designers—people who want space and light, and don't mind if the floor isn't carpeted. Look at this chap . . .'

He turned aside and let me look into a warehouse which had its double doors ajar. A potter was at work, too absorbed to even glance at us.

Darius touched my shoulder lightly, and we moved on to the next open door, through which I could see a small fat woman in dungarees wrestling with a big plaster cast of indeterminate shape.

A little farther on there was a double door painted in

rainbow stripes. Inside, a tall, dark woman was dunking a hank of silk in a beaker of bright orange dye and staring at it critically. Shining cones of coloured silks stood beside a small hand loom. The Lady of Shalott would have had a field day.

We walked on again. The lane curved round to the left, following the line of the river. I could see the water every now and then, since most of the buildings had little side-alleys, like the one at Crispin Wharf House, leading to the riverside. And like the alley beside Crispin Wharf House, most of them had wild flowers growing out of crevices in the walls. Darius was right—Magpie Lane was not at all a grim place once you got to know it.

I stubbed my toe on one of the ancient paving-stones, and he put out his hand to catch me. Then he tucked my arm into his and we walked along together.

I suppose there was nothing really special about Darius, but he had a way of looking at me as though he took me seriously, as though *I* was special. It was a nice feeling.

'Now I wonder . . .' he said, and put his head around another door.

He turned back to me.

'Come on in,' he said. 'It's tea-break time.'

He held the door open for me and I slipped inside.

If Santa Claus ever wanted recruits for his workshop, he'd have found them here. Four elderly men in long white aprons sat drinking strong tea out of enamel mugs, surrounded by bits and pieces of model boats, pots of paint, coils of rope and lengths of red and brown canvas. There was a smell of paint and glue and fresh wood shavings.

Darius introduced me to the four old men, and they made shuffling movements with their feet as though they were going to stand up politely, but somehow they didn't actually do so. I didn't take in their names, I was too busy looking at their faces. One had a ring of ginger curls under a baggy cap, one looked like the captain on a fish-fingers packet, with a stiff fringe of white whiskers round a shiny red face, one wore steel-rimmed spectacles, and one had a face like a knobbly potato.

Darius picked up one of the model boats—a sailing barge with dark red sails.

'Why,' I cried, 'that's just like the Tate and Lyle barge I saw from Philippa's office!'

'Ar,' said Potato Face. 'I went to Dunkirk in one like that.'

'Really?' I said. He looked a bit old for sailing across the Channel. 'Did you—er—did you enjoy it?'

He looked at me as though I was daft.

'*Enjoy* it?' he said. 'Enjoy *Dunkirk*?'

I wondered. Surely he couldn't mean . . .

'When did you go there?' I asked.

'Oh, long time ago now,' he said. 'Ernie, when was Dunkirk?'

'Nineteen-forty,' said Ernie with the steel-rimmed spectacles. 'End of May—early June. *I* went on the *Royal Daffodil . . .*'

'Here she is,' said Darius, showing me a model of a sturdy little steamer. 'Famous for taking people on pleasure cruises . . .'

'Dunkirk wasn't no pleasure cruise,' growled Ernie, and the other old men nodded in agreement, their faces sombre. I felt very small. It was like meeting men who'd sailed against the Armada.

'And didn't Jerry go for us afterwards!' said White Whiskers. 'When did the big bombing start here, Ernie?'

'September nineteen-forty,' said Ernie. 'September seventh, Jerry come over and pasted the docks all night. Everything went up in flames—proper old Brock's Benefit, *that* was.'

'Timber yards at Surrey Docks all ablaze—miles of 'em—and they went on burning for a whole week,' said Ginger.

'Ar,' said Potato Face. 'And Jerry come back the next night . . .'

'*And* the next, *and* the next,' said Ginger.

'Come over every night all through September and October,' said Ernie. 'Regular as clockwork they was. We used to go down to the shelters to sleep, and come up in the morning wondering what we was going to find—if there was anything *to* find . . .'

'King and Queen come to see us,' said Ginger proudly. 'I had my photo took with them.'

'I had my photo took with Churchill when *he* come down here,' said Potato Face.

'I had my photo took with Monty when *he* come here, but there were thousands of us standing all round him— they had him perched up on a crate or something so we could all see him, but I was at the back and all I could see was his black beret—I heard him through the loudspeakers. I was in some of the photos, but all you could see was the back of my head—'

'Them photographers aren't fools,' said Ginger.

'Those were the days,' said White Whiskers, and the four old men sighed.

'Those were the days,' said Ginger.

'After the war, everything seemed to go wrong,' said White Whiskers.

'Started off all right,' said Ernie. 'They rebuilt the docks—things seemed to be going well—but they wasn't.'

'Unions and bosses playing silly buggers,' said Potato Face.

'But they was always doing that,' protested Ginger. 'Must of been more to it than that.'

'The ships just didn't seem to be coming here any more,' said Potato Face. 'Big oil tankers wanted too much room—'

'Them jugginauts took a lot of the trade,' said Ginger.

'The wife's nephew drives one of 'em—container wagons, he calls 'em—picks up a load from a factory in Scotland and drives it all the way to a supermarket warehouse in Germany. 'You can't carry anything like as much in that there jugginaut as ships do," I told him. "Ah," he says, "but I takes it direct from seller to buyer, door-to-door delivery —that's why they like me," he says.'

'Container wagons,' said Ernie contemptuously. 'Going along nose to tail like a bunch of circus elephants . . .'

'Container wagons and container ships,' said Potato Face. His face darkened. 'We could have handled container ships here. No, they have to go and build special terminals for them at Tilbury—'

'*And* Southampton,' said White Whiskers.

'And everywhere,' said Ginger. 'Everywhere but here. Then they said they was going to close London Docks, and we didn't believe 'em.'

''Course we din't believe 'em,' said White Whiskers. 'The docks have been here for hundreds of years . . .'

'And so've we,' said Ginger. 'We've been here *thousands* of years . . .'

'Well, we're still here, aren't we?' said Potato Face belligerently. 'They pay us to make models to put in museums to show people what it was like in the old days.'

'Ar,' said Ginger. 'Wonder they don't put *us* in a museum.'

Ernie stood up.

'Right, lads,' he said. 'Tea-break's over. Back to work. 'Bye, Darius. 'Bye, miss . . .'

Once more there was a general shuffling of feet, but this time the old men stood up, washed out their mugs at the sink in the corner and settled down to work again while Darius and I stepped out into the sunlight again.

Beyond the old men's workshop was an open space where once a warehouse must have stood.

'That looks interesting,' I said.

'People round here call it the Reef Knot Garden,' said

Darius. 'I suppose it all depends on what you think of as a garden . . . Let's go in, shall we?'

We stepped off the worn paving stones of Magpie Lane into the so-called Garden with its smooth modern floor of bright red bricks. It was like standing on the stage of a theatre and looking up at a tiered semi-circle of seats.

'It's like a very small Greek theatre,' I said.

'You've seen some big Greek theatres?' said Darius, smiling.

'Well, I've seen the one they call the Greek theatre at Taormina,' I said. 'You could stand there in the blazing sunshine and look through the stone columns and see Etna in the distance topped with snow. I spent a holiday there a few years ago.'

'Was it a good holiday?' he asked.

Why had I mentioned Taormina, when what I remembered most about the place was going into my bedroom, shuttered against the strong sunlight, leaning back against the door and letting the tears pour down my cheeks because my husband had fallen in love with someone else. It wasn't the first time, but it was the last, because this, Brian told me, was the Real Thing, and I, apparently, was not. In an unbelievably short time we were divorced. Brian married the Real Thing, and soon he was betraying her as once he had betrayed me. And I? Hurt and humiliated, I crept into my Tower of Shalott and shut the door. So—why had I mentioned Taormina to Darius?

'Oh, the place was lovely,' I said.

'That's not quite what I asked,' he said. 'Still, what do you think of the Garden?'

'It's—unexpected,' I said.

A series of shallow steps and ramps led up to the topmost tier, and there, black against the pale blue autumn sky, were three strange shapes. The nearest I can get to describing them is to say that they looked like three very large hourglasses perched upon stilts.

'Those are reef knots,' said Darius. 'Considerably larger than life—made out of twisted ropes and put up to remind everyone of the great ships that used to come here in the old days.'

'But those ropes are as big round as—as a small tree-trunk,' I said. 'Surely none of the ships that came here would be big enough to use cables that size?'

Darius laughed.

'You can't judge everything by the *Silver Swan*,' he said.

'No,' I said. 'But—did they ever have any really big ships here?'

'My dear girl,' said Darius, 'this is the Pool of London! It was a centre of trading ships from—well, from the time of the Romans.'

'"Thousands of years," as Ginger said?' I asked.

'Well, getting on for two thousand, I suppose,' he said. 'Give or take a hundred years. Come and have a look . . .'

I saw now that the tiers of the Garden were flat walkways of narrow brick that could only be reached by a zigzag of steps and ramps. We climbed up the zigzag until we reached the top and looked down over the low brick wall. There below us was the River Thames, sparkling in the afternoon sun.

Darius swung himself up on to the wall, and helped me up beside him.

A few barges covered in black tarpaulin were moored at a jetty downstream to our right, and there were more barges moored in midstream. On the opposite bank were refurbished buff-coloured warehouses looking like Venetian palazzi, and away upstream to our left I could see the blue and white of Tower Bridge, and beyond it the gold cross on the dome of St Paul's.

I looked down at the water hurrying away to the sea.

'Is it very deep here?' I asked.

'"Full fathom five," I think,' said Darius. 'That's at high tide—say thirty feet—about as high as a house.'

'Is it high tide now?' I asked.

'No, the water comes up very much higher,' he said. 'You can see the high water mark on the wall—you'll have to lean back a bit—careful, you don't want to fall in.'

I leaned back and he put his arm round me to steady me. I spotted the high water mark quite quickly, but he kept his arm round me, which was very comforting. One or two small boats moved busily up and down, some gulls swooped about, and a helicopter buzzed noisily over our heads and then was gone. We seemed to have the Thames to ourselves.

'How broad the river is here,' I said. 'But—how empty it is!'

'Two hundred years ago,' said Darius, 'you wouldn't have been able to see the far bank at all because of the forest of masts and rigging on the ships loading and unloading here.'

'It doesn't seem possible now,' I said.

'Even in mediæval times it was a busy place,' he said. 'Everybody and everything came here—grain, timber, spices, wine, wool—did you know that Chaucer was a kind of Customs Inspector for the wool trade?'

'Was he really?' I said. 'Did he work round here somewhere?'

'He'd have had an office on the other bank, near the Tower of London,' said Darius. 'But he must have known all this area pretty well.'

'Why, of course!' I said. 'His Canterbury Pilgrims began their journey in Southwark—that's just up the road from here, isn't it?'

He nodded.

'And the Pilgrim Fathers started their journey here in Rotherhithe,' he said, and waited for me to swallow the bait.

'But the Pilgrim Fathers started from Plymouth!' I cried. 'That's why they called their landing place Plymouth Rock. Everybody knows that!'

'They put into Plymouth for repairs,' he said. 'But the

Mayflower actually began its voyage here—probably only a few hundred yards away . . .'

'The *Mayflower* . . .' I said. Somehow I'd never associated the Pilgrim Fathers with London.

'Their navigator's buried in the Parish Church here,' said Darius. 'Mind you, he can't have been very good at his job, since he took them to Cape Cod when they wanted to go to Virginia. Still, at least he navigated himself back here safely.'

'But—what happened to all the big ships?' I said. 'I mean, the modern versions of them, the ones the old men were talking about?'

'Well,' said Darius, 'I'm not all that good at history, but I think it went something like this. In the eighteen-hundreds they built lots of big docks to take the big ships of the day. Everything was flourishing—Industrial Revolution, heyday of the British Empire, and all that.'

I nodded.

'But by the nineteen-twenties,' said Darius, 'things were not so good. The sun was setting on the British Empire, and of course there was the Depression.'

He looked at me questioningly.

'Yes,' I said, 'I *have* heard of the Depression.'

'Then came World War Two,' said Darius. 'The Luftwaffe bombed the docks to smithereens—well, you heard what Ginger and Ernie said.'

'But didn't Ernie say that the docks were rebuilt after the war?'

'Yes, they were,' he said. 'Rebuilt, enlarged, improved.'

'Then—why . . .?' I said, looking at the empty stretch of water.

'Well, for one thing,' said Darius, 'a lot of other people were busy improving and enlarging their docks—think of Rotterdam and Antwerp just across the Channel. And then container ships arrived in the 'sixties—just about the time that you and I were born.'

He smiled at me, as though it was an extraordinary coincidence that we had been born about the same time. I had a sudden vision of Darius as though I was looking at a series of snapshots—Darius as a solemn little boy in his first school uniform, Darius in a bright yellow life-jacket sailing a dinghy, Darius as a student in cap and gown. But then—what? What had led him into his present life with its trips to Marrakech and Karachi and wherever it was?

'Anyhow, somebody decided they didn't need the docks and warehouses round here any more, and in the 'seventies they closed the London Docks and put everything up for sale. Then the oil crisis in 1973 knocked the bottom out of the property market . . .'

'Philippa said something about warehouses going cheap a few years ago,' I said. 'I hadn't realized what had happened here. It must have been—desolate.'

Darius nodded.

'Things are starting to move now,' he said.

'Developers?' I said.

He nodded again.

'The really big warehouses on both sides of the river are being turned into hotels and offices and flats. They'll probably put up some terrace houses in Crispin Wharf Street before long. You're seeing the place now at an in-between stage. Heaven knows how much of Magpie Lane will survive.'

The mention of Crispin Wharf Street reminded me of something which had been puzzling me.

'Where did you leave the *Silver Swan*?' I asked. 'I can't see it anywhere.'

'There's a small channel on the far side of Crispin Wharf House,' said Darius. 'Just big enough to take it.'

'I don't remember seeing a channel,' I said doubtfully. 'Wouldn't I have seen it as I walked down Crispin Wharf Street?'

'Did you notice a curtain of greenery stretching from Crispin Wharf House to a builder's yard?'

'Yes. Yes, I did see that.'

'The channel is on the other side of the green curtain,' said Darius. 'The *Silver Swan* is certainly very useful round here. I took Mary to the television studios this afternoon—or rather Mary took me—I'm teaching her to handle the boat—and Julian came along for the ride. Philippa sometimes takes him to the piers at Westminster or Charing Cross.'

'So Philippa can handle a boat?' I said.

'Is there anything Philippa can't handle?' said Darius, and he laughed. 'I don't think old Julian's ever going to get the hang of it, but then I don't think he really wants to—he's too used to having Philippa doing everything for him. Do you live near the river, Astolat?'

I shook my head.

'Not really,' I said. 'But I live at Blackheath, so I'm not that far from the river at Greenwich. I've got a little flat. The first novel I ever sold was about a romantic highwayman who roamed about Blackheath. Of course at that time I'd never even seen Blackheath, but I thought it sounded wonderful.'

'And did you acquire your flat on the proceeds?'

'Good heavens, no!' I said. 'The book didn't bring in enough to pay the phone bill. No, I had to wait quite a few years before I got my flat.'

'Do you live on your own?' he asked.

'Yes,' I said.

'No family?'

'Only my grandmother. She lives in a village in Sussex.'

'And do you still write about romantic highwaymen?'

'No,' I said. 'I know now they weren't romantic at all. Just a bunch of thugs.'

I plucked up my courage. Darius wasn't the only one who could ask personal questions.

'And what about you?' I said. 'Where do you live?'

'At the moment,' he said, 'I'm staying at the Magpie Inn down the lane.'

'What—the old black and white pub?' I said, surprised. He nodded.

'Said to be the haunt of smugglers in the old days,' he said. 'It's my guess that practically *anywhere* round here would have been the haunt of smugglers in the old days. Do you find smugglers romantic, Astolat?'

'No,' I said. 'No more romantic than highwaymen . . .'

He looked at me searchingly, and my heart began to thump quite unreasonably.

'And next week,' he said, 'I'm off to Marrakech again.'

My heart stopped thumping.

How long would he be out there? When would he be coming back? *Would* he be coming back? In other words, would I ever see him again? I couldn't ask the only questions that really mattered.

'Come on,' he said. 'I'd better get you to your bus stop.'

He helped me down from my perch on the wall and I followed him down the zigzag of steps and ramps. As we reached street level I noticed a heap of cables in one corner, with a long iron bar poking up in the air like a giant knitting needle stuck into a Brobdingnagian skein of wool, and supported by an old red oil drum. I stooped down and tried to lift one of the cables. I couldn't move it an inch.

'It must weigh a ton!' I said. 'I'd no idea rope was so heavy.'

Darius bent down and tugged at the cable. *He* couldn't move it either.

'It's not just rope,' he said. 'Look, the cables are twisted round a core of iron—you can see they've come untwisted from that iron bar resting on the oil drum, otherwise the iron would run right through them. No wonder you couldn't shift it.'

I ran my hand over the thick strands of rope, and gave a

yelp of pain as a broken fibre ran into my finger, sharp as a needle. I put my hand to my mouth and sucked at the painful spot.

'It looked so lovely and smooth,' I said ruefully.

'Didn't I tell you that you can't always judge by appearances?' said Darius, in a voice of mock solemnity.

I smiled up at him.

There was sudden harsh shriek, and a band of black shadow covered his eyes like a highwayman's mask. It was gone in a second. Darius looked up and laughed.

'Only a gull,' he said.

With strong wings outstretched, a grey and white bird floated above us, sending its shadow skimming over the red brickwork. The white wings flapped, and the gull wheeled and disappeared behind the three reef knots.

I shivered, and moved quickly out of the Reef Knot Garden into the friendlier surroundings of Magpie Lane.

CHAPTER 5

'HAVE A NICE DAY ...'

The next day I went on a shopping expedition. When I joined the Crispin Speakers' Agency I hadn't anticipated having to fork out for expensive clothes—certainly not before I'd given my first talk and received my first cheque. But I saw the force of Philippa's argument—my audiences (if any) would expect me to conform to their idea of what a romantic novelist looks like, and I'd better not disappoint them. And I could afford to lash out a bit. My bank balance was healthy, and I had just received a very satisfactory cheque from my publishers for my June royalties. (Yes, I know it was now October, but that's the way my publishers work. June royalties arrive in October, and December royalties arrive about Easter. Once you get into the system it's all right, but the first couple of years can be difficult.) I had been thinking of buying a rather expensive word-processor to replace my golf-ball typewriter, but perhaps clothes were more important. They might even be more fun. (And Darius might come back from Marrakech . . .) All the same, Bambinetta would be expensive, so I worked out exactly how much I was prepared to spend.

But first I was going to buy all three of Darius Underwood's books. I went into my usual bookshop and asked for them.

'Do you have—or can you get—*Anatolian Notebook, Karachi Notebook* and *Modern Marrakech: A Notebook*?' I asked. 'They're all by Darius Underwood.'

'I don't know the name,' said the assistant doubtfully. 'Who is the publisher?'

'I'm sorry, I don't know,' I said.

'I'll see if I can trace them on microfiche,' she offered, only to come back apologizing, 'I've tried under D for Darius as well as under U for Underwood, but we don't have any record of the author. Do you know the date of publication?'

'No,' I said. 'But they must be fairly recent—within the last few years.'

'If you can find out the date, or the publisher,' she said. 'Or they might turn up as remainders somewhere . . .'

I tried several bookshops, and drew blank at each one, and for the first time I began to wonder if Darius had paid a publisher to bring out his work. This is something all self-respecting, self-supporting authors deplore, since of course we expect publishers to pay us, not the other way round. We quote horror stories of unscrupulous gentlemen who advertise offers to print your work, and then do precisely that. They print the pages—but they do not collate them, or bind them, or put covers on them—and they certainly do not attempt to sell them, so that the unhappy author is left with a depleted wallet and a stack of paper suitable for use as very expensive firelighters. Poets, of course, often have to pay to have their slim volumes published, and this we do not deplore, because we realize that poetry by unknown authors rarely makes money for its publishers, and anyway very few of us write poetry.

At the last bookshop I visited I bought a copy of the latest work by the Contessa della Stola, a fellow novelist, i.e. a rival. Nothing by the Contessa could possibly be classified as poetry, but I like to keep an eye on the competition.

The bookshop was in the Charing Cross Road, and it occurred to me that Bamba's Dress Hire was somewhere near. It would be sensible to call in and have a look at it before going to Bambinetta's salon de haute couture. As Philippa had said, if Bambinetta's prices were as high as her couture, then I could go down-market and hire some clothes from Bamba instead.

I found Bamba's Dress Hire quite quickly, in a cul-de-sac off the Charing Cross Road, a sunless courtyard of tall grey buildings not unlike Crispin Wharf House. The autumn wind chased bits of paper and plastic and dry brown leaves along the pavement, and piled them up at the far end of the courtyard.

Underneath Bamba's there was a nightclub in the basement, reached by steps going down into a railed area with a couple of overflowing dustbins and a spindly shrub in a tub. A lot of unswept sweepings were down there too. A scruffy nightclub. (I would have called it a cheap nightclub but that would be a contradiction in terms.)

But Bamba's Dress Hire was bright and cheerful, with a large window displaying a wedding group of smiling bride, bridesmaids big and small, bride's mother, bride's pet dog and—oh yes, the bridegroom, half-hidden behind a floral display.

I walked up three broad steps, pushed open the heavy glass door and met a gush of warm air and the sound of muzak. I walked past several displays of dresses, some of which I recognized as having been worn at the Royal Casterbridge Hotel by the mynah birds.

The receptionist smiled at me brightly.

'Good morning, madam, how may I help you?' she said. I felt ridiculously bashful.

'C-can I have a copy of your p-price list? I said.

'My pleasure, madam,' she said, and handed me a leaflet. 'Would you like to see anything in particular—wedding, barmitzvah, country house party—' she paused, and then breathed—'*investiture*?'

'Oh, I don't need anything at the moment,' I said. 'It's just that I m-may—I may need something fairly soon.' Why did I feel it necessary to explain things?) I felt myself blushing as I spoke.

'Weddings are our speciality,' said the receptionist encouragingly, which didn't help my blushes in the least.

'Thanks,' I muttered, and fled out into the street.

'Have a nice day . . .' she called after me, and then the door closed.

Immediately opposite Bamba's there was a coffee-shop with three coffee-mills twirling around and releasing their wonderful, irresistible fragrance. I went in, ordered myself a coffee and a couple of croissants, and sat down at a table in the window. Then I took out the leaflet which bore the bright heading:

BAMBA'S DRESS HIRE
WE CAN FIT ANY BODY

I was buttering my first croissant when I noticed the door in the basement had opened. Somebody was coming out of the nightclub and slowly climbing up the steep steps to the street.

A fat old woman wearing a shapeless black dress heaved

herself up the steps, gripping the iron railings for support.
I could imagine her wheezing and puffing as she climbed.
At the top of the steps she paused and looked round. I could
see now that she was squat, almost square. Her face was
white, as white as a clown's, and she was wearing an odd
hat like a black beehive—or was it long black hair swathed
tightly round her head? It was the nightclub cleaner coming
off duty. She went up the three broad steps into Bamba's
Dress Hire. Probably she worked there as well as in the
nightclub. If she'd been going there to hire a dress she would
present them with quite a problem. WE CAN FIT ANY BODY,
they said. They'd have a job with her . . .

I dipped into the Contessa novel and found, as I had
expected, that she had written the same novel yet again.
She has to date written at least thirty novels, and the only
difference between them that I have ever seen has been in
the names of the characters and the settings in which they
find themselves, since the characters (and it is flattering to
call them that) perform exactly the same actions and speak
exactly the same dialogue. (All right, so I am a little jealous
of the Contessa.)

I was eating my second croissant when the door of
Bamba's Dress Hire opened. The bright receptionist was
holding it open for the old woman with the black beehive
on her head. But she was no longer the old woman who had
climbed so slowly up the steps from the nightclub. Now she
was a figure of importance and power. She wore a full-length
mink coat and swept down the three broad steps like an
empress. I took off my hat to Bamba's Dress Hire. They
could indeed, as they claimed, fit any body.

I wondered who the old woman was and my novelist's
imagination came into play. Could she be a nightclub
cleaner who had spent a month's pay on a smart outfit so
as not to disgrace her son or daughter who was getting
married—no, not married, she was wearing a black dress
under the mink. Perhaps her husband was having a retire-

ment presentation—no, not at that time in the morning. Well, perhaps somebody in her family had been awarded a medal for outstanding bravery and she was going to Buckingham Palace for the investiture. I could make quite a nice story out of her . . .

It was time to be on my way to Bambinetta's. It was a fine sunny morning—what my grandmother refers to as St Luke's Summer—and I decided to walk to Mayfair, cutting through the dingy back streets of Soho, crossing Regent Street and Bond Street—going up-market all the way— and then heading for Weaver's Row, a street of tall, narrow houses, all faced in pink terracotta and decorated with terracotta balconies and Dutch gables. Bambinetta was the last house in Weaver's Row, and beyond it I could see a small mews. Bambinetta's name-plate was so discreet that I almost walked right past it. The house had a window which displayed a single evening gown against a background of ivory drapes, and a white door. I told myself firmly that it was only a shop, and went in.

The foyer looked and smelled very expensive. Ivory walls, ivory drapes, and an ivory carpet that was deep and soft like freshly fallen snow. (But what did they do if it really was snowing, and their customers had wet or muddy shoes?) The room was narrower than I had expected, but it went back quite a long way. Tucked into an arch facing the door was a charming little secretaire complete with ivory telephone and a smiling blonde receptionist so cool she might have been sculptured out of ice-cream. I gave her Philippa's card.

'Ah—you are a friend of Miss Preston? One moment, please . . .'

She had a slight foreign accent, and I thought of her as Scandinavian.

She picked up the ivory telephone.

'Madame Bamba? I have at Reception a young lady who is a friend of Miss Preston—Miss Elaine Astolat . . . yes, she has a card from Miss Preston . . . I will bring it at once, Madame . . .'

She rang off and turned to me.

'Please take a seat, Miss Astolat . . . Madame will be here immediately . . .'

(So Madame Bamba herself was coming to see me. Philippa's card was an Open Sesame. Without it I should never have been so honoured. What it was to be on the Old Gals' network . . .)

The receptionist indicated a couch, and then disappeared through the room beyond the archway. There must be a door somewhere, although I couldn't see one. All I could see at the far end was a wall of mirrors which showed me my own reflection looking slightly ill at ease in such elegant surroundings. I turned towards the couch. It was made of polished wood with a padded seat of ivory silk and two cylindrical cushions with long silken tassels reaching almost to the floor. Close to the couch—so close that when I was seated I could easily touch it—was a small table on which were displayed expensive little trifles of jade and ivory, some pretty silver brooches and a pair of ear-rings in glowing red amber. I was surprised to find them laid out with so little protection against theft. It would have been a simple matter to slip any one of them into my handbag—especially as the receptionist was not there to keep an eye on them, and on me. Perhaps they were guarded by a photo-electric eye? I didn't propose to find out. I was quite nervous enough without touching anything that might set off alarm bells.

I sat quietly looking around the room, storing up my impressions. They would come in handy whenever I wrote a story in which the heroine visits a dress salon—and I would see to it that one of my heroines did so in the near future. I could hear music coming faintly from one of the upper floors. Debussy? Ravel? Something ethereal, far removed from the cheerful muzak of the sister establishment off the Charing Cross Road. Then, as Madame Bamba seemed to be taking her time, I decided I might as well write my impressions down while I was waiting. I took out my copy of the Contessa's novel, and was about to use it as a desk on which to rest my notebook when the wall of mirror-glass slid noiselessly to one side, revealing the fine gilded lattice-work of an old-fashioned lift-gate. The lattice-work was pushed aside by an imperious hand and a woman stepped out of the lift and came towards me. A woman in black, a fat woman with a dead-white face and shining long black hair swathed around her head in the shape of a beehive. She paused in the doorway.

'Miss Astolat? I am Madame Bamba...'

It was the old woman from Bamba's Dress Hire. Not a nightclub cleaner, but the owner of Bamba's Dress Hire and Bambinetta Haute Couture. It was strange that I hadn't heard the lift arriving. The noiseless sliding of the mirror-glass wall had been the first indication of Madame Bamba's presence.

She walked through the archway and came towards me, majestic in black velvet and a long rope of freshwater pearls. We shook hands. Her nails were painted blood-red, and they were as sharp as talons. I tried not to look at them.

'How do you do?' I said, feeling as awkward as a school-girl.

'Miss Preston sends you to me to buy some romantic clothes,' said Madame Bamba. 'She sends you to the right person. I dress many romantic ladies. I dress Mary Michaelmas—you have seen her on television, perhaps?'

'Yes, I have seen her,' I said. 'I saw her at the Royal Casterbridge Hotel. She was wearing a dress of mauve and silver lace.'

Madame Bamba smiled. 'Ah, is one of mine,' she said. 'Mary Michaelmas is very lovely, and always she wear very lovely clothes...'

(Philippa Preston must have telephoned Madame Bamba

about my need for romantic clothes. There was nothing on her card to indicate what I wanted. My respect for Philippa's thoroughness increased.)

'I see you have a book by the Contessa della Stola,' said Madame Bamba. 'She is very romantic—just like her books . . . A sweet little lady, the body of a woman and the heart of a child!'

And the writing ability of a hamster! I thought.

(You may have gathered by now that it is inadvisable to praise one romantic writer to another until you are sure of your ground. In many cases it is the modern equivalent of telling Elizabeth Tudor of your admiration for Mary Stuart.)

'And Miss Preston tells me that you write too . . .' she said.

'*You write too . . .*'

I wanted to shout out, 'I am Elaine Astolat, the successful writer of romantic novels—and very much better ones than the Contessa's!' But then this was the very purpose of the exercise—to dress myself in such a way that everyone would recognize me at once as a romantic writer—and what is more, a successful romantic writer who could afford to patronize Madame Bamba's expensive establishment.

'And I think,' added Madame Bamba, putting her head on one side like the early bird sighting a worm, 'I think there is a young man also, no?'

Her little black eyes twinkled roguishly at me and I felt myself blushing. She smiled broadly.

'Ah-ha,' she said, 'I can always tell. You have a—a certain glow. Is very becoming. And now—*parlons chiffons* —we talk about clothes, no? Mademoiselle Chantal will assist you to make your choice. It will not be easy . . . I have so many romantic dresses . . . very beautiful . . . you will want them all, I am sure. Now, because you are a friend of Miss Preston, and because you have that certain glow— I make you special price for any dresses you choose.'

She led me towards the lift and I stepped inside. It was an elegant affair, its polished wood cage decorated with curlicues and sinuous vine leaves—a relic of Edwardian days. I turned round to face her, looking for the control buttons.

'No, no,' said Madame Bamba. 'The buttons they are on the other side of the lift . . . you will get out on that side on the second floor, and you will find Mademoiselle Chantal awaiting you. Goodbye, my dear Miss Astolat. A pleasure to meet you. I shall look forward to your next visit, no?'

'Goodbye, Madame,' I said.

The mirror-door in the wall closed without a sound, and then the lift-gates whispered shut. I turned to push the control button, but as I did so I dropped the Contessa's book on the floor behind me. I swung round to pick it up, and my hand accidentally caught one of the wooden curlicues. To my astonishment it slipped back silently to disclose a tiny peephole through which I could see the whole of the room that I had just left. Madame Bamba was standing by the couch looking at the display of elegant little trifles. For an uncomfortable moment I wondered if, when I was waiting for her, she had been standing here, watching me as I was now watching her. It was possible that the lift could be entered from the back so that Madame could take a look at her customers before they saw her. There had been absolutely no sound of a lift arriving, of that I was quite sure. So if the lift made a sound, however slight, on its upward journey, then I could be sure that Madame had been spying on me. It was not a nice feeling. I was glad I had not touched any of the expensive trifles.

I pressed the button for the second floor, and the lift ascended with a pleasant humming sound. So Madame *had* been using the peephole to spy on me. But why?

I had no time to think that one out. The lift hummed to a gentle stop and Mademoiselle Chantal awaited me, a thin, middle-aged blonde in a dress of pale, creamy wool.

'Miss Astolat? I am Mademoiselle Chantal. Madame Bamba tells me you are someone very special . . . you are a friend of Miss Preston, no?'

'That's right,' I said, and once more I thanked Philippa Preston for smoothing my path. Even so, faced with so much elegance, I once more felt like an awkward schoolgirl.

The room was larger than the one downstairs, and full-length mirrors on the walls made it look even larger. There were shell-shaped chairs covered in rose-pink velvet, white wallpaper sprinkled with tiny pink rosebuds—I didn't need to be told that this was the Bambinetta equivalent of the Bridal Suite.

'Madame will make you a special price because you are a friend of Miss Preston,' said Mademoiselle Chantal. 'But first, please, you tell me how much you want to spend . . .'

I named a figure which seemed high enough to me, but which caused Mademoiselle Chantal to give a tiny wince of pain, bravely covered. I wondered how much her customers usually spent, and how much her commission was.

'Ah, I see you read the Contessa's book!' cried Mademoiselle Chantal, as I put the book down on one of the shell-like chairs. 'She is a sweet person. She buys many beautiful clothes—she is not my client, you understand, but I see her often. She has signed one of her books for me—a sweet woman . . .'

Minions began to arrive bearing romantic dresses and I began to try them on.

The first one was a pretty fair disaster—a black velvet bodice over short puffed sleeves and a full, a very full, skirt. I looked like Snow White—and she's well past her fiftieth birthday. I said so. Mademoiselle Chantal was sad.

But not for long. A couple of adorable updated 'twenties dresses appeared, shimmering with tiny beads and silk fringing. Mademoiselle Chantal was enchanted. I looked at my reflection in a dozen mirrors and was equally enchanted.

But—were they really 'romantic'? Were they what 'my public' would expect to see? I put the question to Mademoiselle Chantal, and she sent for more dresses.

Before long, the room was filled with clouds of tulle and chiffon, as though the entire corps de ballet of *Les Sylphides* had flown by overhead, disrobing as they went, and I was whirling around in a flutter of frills and flounces. I looked at the mirrors, and saw a hundred Astolats rising out of a foam of petticoats, while a hundred Mademoiselle Chantals knelt in adoration.

I could feel myself becoming a woman of some importance. And why not? I asked myself. I *am* a woman of some importance. I am Elaine Astolat, the successful novelist . . .

Mademoiselle Chantal came in carrying a filmy pink confection with crystal-pleated sleeves. I knew at once that it was made for me. I slipped it on, raised my arms and the sleeves floated me up to heaven.

It was, of course, an utterly impractical dress for luncheon and supper club engagements—the sleeves alone would make it impossible to tackle the soup course, but—what an entrance I should make! How gracefully I could pick up a book and hold my audience spellbound as I read to them, or rather, pretended to read to them, as Philippa had counselled me.

Mademoiselle Chantal was ecstatic, but she had an eye to business. A minion arrived bringing yet more frilly petticoats, this time topped with crimson velvet. With a sigh I permitted Mademoiselle Chantal to assist me out of the pink dress. The crimson velvet looked very dashing, but it was not going to usurp the place in my heart that belonged to the pink one. I stepped into the frilly white petticoat, and as I moved I heard for the first time that most seductive of sounds—*frou-frou . . . frou-frou . . . frou-frou . . .* None of the other frilly petticoats had made that delightful sound. Over the petticoats went a bell skirt of crimson velvet, and a tight-fitting jacket with little gold buttons. Delicate lace ruffles swooned over my hands. I looked like a highly romanticized picture of a Victorian lady in skating costume.

'Anna Karenina!' cried Mademoiselle Chantal. 'Camille! Scarlett O'Hara!'

And she was right. This was the romantic dress to end all romantic dresses. I had to have it. But then I had to have the pink dress with the wonderful sleeves.

Mademoiselle Chantal made a slight, a very slight, inclination of her head, and the minions departed. We were alone together. And suddenly I saw her, not as the Mademoiselle Chantal who had knelt at my feet in adoration, but as Mademoiselle Chantal, a matador moving in for the kill.

I sighed and slipped off the crimson velvet. The petticoats whispered to me, but I put them firmly aside. And as I did so I put away my romantic dreamy self. I put on my coffee-coloured suit and came back to the real world.

'How much do these two dresses come to?' I asked, indicating the crimson velvet and the pink crystal-pleated one.

'Just the two?' asked Mademoiselle Chantal, the temptress. Her eyes strayed to the shimmering 'twenties dresses, then strayed back to me again.

'Just the two,' I said.

Mademoiselle Chantal produced a tiny pocket calculator and played a rapid cadenza upon it. She turned to me with an apologetic smile.

'It is a little more than you had in mind,' she said, 'but I am sure you will find they are worth the little extra . . .'

'How much?' I said.

Mademoiselle Chantal breathed a figure which was exactly twice the amount I had mentioned to her.

Perfidious woman! 'A *little* more,' she had said. 'The *little* extra . . .'

'Oh dear,' I said, 'that's much more than I intended to spend . . .'

Mademoiselle Chantal was desolated. She ran her fingers caressingly over the crimson velvet, she touched the crystal pleats and let them fall, oh so gently, over my hand.

We were both silent for a little while.

'I think,' murmured Mademoiselle Chantal at last, 'I think—no, I am sure—Madame Bamba would be happy to offer you—facilities . . .'

She looked at me tenderly, and made a soft cooing sound.

I don't like being cooed over, especially by rapacious ladies. And I didn't like the sound of those 'facilities'. I had a picture of Madame Bamba watching me through the peephole in the lift. And I had a picture of those sharp red talons of hers. Decidedly, I was not going to place myself under any kind of obligation to Madame Bamba.

I gave a little sigh. I think I did it rather well.

'I shall just have to do without the word-processor for a little longer.'

Mademoiselle Chantal looked completely disorientated. I don't suppose she had ever equated a lovely dress with a bit of office equipment. I don't suppose she was pleased to lose the chance of the 'facilities'—perhaps she got a commission on them too.

But I was no longer the awkward schoolgirl she had met stepping out of the lift, and I was no longer the dreamy romantic who had whirled around the room in a flutter of frills and flounces. Thanks to her, and her lovely dresses, I was Elaine Astolat, the successful romantic novelist, and I was conscious of my own worth. I had made up my mind to buy those dresses, and I was going to have them without any 'facilities' hanging round my neck. I took out my cheque-book . . .

I left Bambinetta's in a state of great elation. Not only had I acquired two gorgeous dresses, and a whole new personality to go with them, but I had done so within the budget I had set myself, which was twice the amount I had mentioned to Mademoiselle Chantal. I almost danced down the steps into Weaver's Row.

As I walked away I caught sight of something like a flag waving in the breeze. I turned, and saw that it was a swinging metal sign for a nightclub housed in Bambinetta's basement and called The Spider's Web. The name struck me as entirely appropriate.

CHAPTER 6

FIRST STEPS

When the time came for my first engagement as a speaker, I knew my talk and my readings off by heart (although I tucked a copy of them into my make-up bag as a safety-net). I wore the crimson velvet dress, and I was full of confidence as I sailed into the hotel where the luncheon club was meeting.

A large lady was waiting for me with a large gin and tonic, which she placed in my hand as she piloted me to the bar, where some forty or fifty ladies of some forty or fifty years were gathered. The crimson velvet made a splendid impression, and I knew everything was going to be all right. Gin is not my favourite drink, and I quietly deposited the glass, untouched, upon a convenient table, thinking that it would be unnoticed in the crush. But a shaky hand shot out and removed it, and a few minutes later the glass reappeared, empty, so I acquired a quite undeserved reputation as a lady who could hold her liquor.

I was introduced to Madam President, and Madam President introduced me to her committee. She then led me in to lunch (or rather, luncheon—she was most particular about that), and we made polite conversation. She confided that she had often thought of writing, but had never had the time. I asked what kind of writing she had in mind. She told me, blushing slightly, and I thought it was just as well she was kept busy with other matters.

As we reached the coffee stage I suddenly realized what I was doing there. I was about to stand up and talk to all these ladies for an hour—a whole hour! And my mind was a blank!

My throat felt dry. The hand holding my coffee-cup felt damp. Had I got time to dive into my make-up bag and fish out the speech and the readings?

I had not.

Madam President was introducing me—'someone who needs no introduction, since many of us feel we know her already through her lovely books—Miss Elaine Astolat!'

Applause.

Faces turned towards me expectantly.

I stood up, trembling.

'Madam P-President, and ladies—it g-gives me great p-pleasure to be with you today . . .'

And to my utter astonishment, the words that I'd rehearsed so many times came welling up without any conscious effort on my part—which was just as well, because by that time I was beyond making any conscious effort. But I waltzed through my talk as though I'd been doing it for years. I read a passage from *My Dear Cath*, and finished with the last four lines of the Shakespeare sonnet.

Enthusiastic applause.

I sat down, well pleased with myself.

Madam President rose and looked around the room, smiling.

'And now,' she said, 'are there any questions? Rosemary? Shelagh?'

Questions? Panic stations! I had quite forgotten the custom of following a talk with a barrage of questions just to prove that the audience is still awake. I was completely unprepared, and I cursed my lack of foresight.

Rosemary—or perhaps it was Shelagh—was getting to her feet. She asked me a simple question. So, a few minutes later, did Shelagh, or perhaps it was Rosemary. I breathed a little more freely. Questions like these I could cope with.

Then a lady at a far table asked, 'Could you tell us, Miss Astolat, how you actually write your books?'

I opened my mouth to answer, and shut it again. Just in time I heard the voice of the Fretful Porpentine at the Royal Casterbridge reception criticizing the historical novelist as she described her working methods. 'Makes it sound as dull as working for the Gas Board . . .' And something about not wanting to know how the beans got into the can . . .

I abandoned my first impulse to describe the steady routine of a working day, and spoke instead about the joy of seeing the story unroll before me in my imagination, and of sitting quietly as those shadowy creatures, my characters, come alive and begin talking to me. As I spoke, I realized this was a far truer picture of how I write than the stock response of slogging away at the typewriter. Would I have stuck at the job all these years if it had been no more than that? Of course not. But it took a question from a stranger at a luncheon club to bring it home to me.

Then came several questions about books I had written several years ago and had all but forgotten. It was embarrassing to find that my readers remembered details of them better than I did myself. I made a mental note to re-read all my books before I gave another talk.

The last question came from a very old lady.

'Have you red freckles, Miss Astolat?' she asked.

I looked at her in utter astonishment. She didn't look the sort of woman to ask such a personal question. Then a long-forgotten name surged up into my memory. *Freckles, A Girl of the Limberlost* . . . You can't hear capital letters, but what the old lady had actually asked me was, 'Have you read *Freckles*, Miss Astolat?'

'By—er—Gene Stratton Porter?' I said.

The old lady's face lit up.

'I read that story when I was at school,' she said. 'Freckles is one of my favourite heroines. I thought your Olwen Rhys was a bit like her . . .'

I expressed my pleasure at the comparison, and decided to bone up on writers of a much earlier age. It seemed that *Romantic Novelists Today* could cover a wider time-span than I had anticipated.

And that was it. Vote of thanks, proposed by Shelagh and seconded by Rosemary, or possibly the other way about, and it was all over.

I'd done it!

I was approached by a little woman who slipped an envelope into my hand, gave me an embarrassed smile, whispered 'Your fee and expenses,' and disappeared. Philippa had warned me to check before leaving the club that my expenses were covered—but how did I do that? Even in my present state of euphoria I hadn't the nerve to slit the envelope and peek at the cheque in front of everybody.

But what did the money matter?

I'd had a lovely time.

These were lovely people.

They *liked* me.

The Lady of Shalott had broken out of her tower and was having herself a ball.

God bless Philippa Preston and the Crispin Speakers' Agency!

That evening I switched on the radio and renewed my acquaintance with the real Lady of Shalott.

'On either side the river lie.
Long fields of barley and of rye . . .'

It was the start of Julian Leigh's recording, the one that Philippa had mentioned when I visited her at Crispin Wharf House. Julian was the perfect reader for the poem: mellifluous and stately. But what had happened to the passionate young man who had electrified Bettesham theatregoers in the 'fifties, and who had swept the star of Bettesham Rep off her feet? Romeo was now an elderly man leading a comfortable life as the head of the Crispin Speakers' Agency, while Juliet was the presenter of a weekly TV chat show called *Tea with Mary Michaelmas*.

I followed Philippa's advice and watched Mary's show occasionally, just to study her technique. The programme began with a title sequence overlaid with syrupy theme music, then a shot of Mary's hands (complete with amethyst ring) pouring tea. Then a shot of Mary introducing the programme, then a shot of her guest, and then a kind of extended Wimbledon rally as the cameras showed first one and then the other.

On one occasion Mary had a terribly nervous guest, whose hand shook so much that the teaspoon in her saucer rattled against the cup like an alarm bell. Smiling, Mary leaned across the table and gently removed the cup from the lady's hand. It was a graceful and kindly gesture, although the movement took the camera operator by surprise, since usually Mary and her guest sat perfectly still, as though they were strapped into their seats.

Mary herself always looked and sounded quite delightful: her silver curls bobbed merrily as she put her guests at their ease, twinkled at their jokes and generally supported them. If her guest was a candle-maker or an expert on pot plants, Mary said the very thing to enable him or her to shine. It looked easy, but after I'd seen one or two shows I realized that Mary was a perfect example of the art that conceals art.

I noticed that quite a number of her guests were members

of the Crispin Speakers' Agency, and I wondered if this was merely coincidence.

At the end of November I spent a week's holiday with my grandmother at her home in Sussex. She always watches Mary's show.

'I like Mary Michaelmas,' said my grandmother. 'She may not be a clever woman, but she's clever enough to have grown old gracefully. She's let her hair turn silver, and very pretty she looks too.' (As she spoke, my grandmother's hand unconsciously smoothed her own pretty white hair.)

We watched the beginning of *Tea with Mary Michaelmas*. The guest was an actress who had recently made a hit on TV playing a character who was a one-woman firework display of witty remarks. I wondered how she and Mary would get on, and as I glanced at the opening titles I sensed that they probably would not get on at all. For the first time ever, as far as I knew, Mary's show began, not with Mary's hands pouring tea, but with Mary's guest making a grand entrance, twirling to show the camera a practically backless skin-tight dress before taking her seat and her mandatory cup of tea. But after that the show seemed to be settling down into its well-oiled groove. Then my grandmother gave a sudden snort of disgust.

'The silly woman!' she exclaimed. 'She's trying to put Mary Michaelmas down. How very ill-bred! And she's pretending to be in her early forties! Why, she must be almost as old as I am. Just listen to her . . .'

I heard the star give a silvery laugh and say, 'Mary, darling, I'm afraid I can't remember *quite* as far back as you can . . .'

Mary was not being upstaged on her own show. Her smile never faltered, but she quietly abandoned the prepared questions on her clipboard and began to ask unrehearsed ones. Without a scriptwriter to supply her with witty remarks, the star floundered, and then foundered. Mary went on smiling sweetly, but there was no doubt that she was putting the boot in. At the end of the programme the camera crept towards her as she made her closing announcement and added straight to camera, 'This is the first time we've met since we appeared together as the Babes in the Wood—' and here she gave a broad grin and a hint of a wink—'and I daren't tell you how long ago *that* was . . .'

There was a shriek of rage from the offscreen guest, covered immediately by the syrupy theme music which played while the end titles rolled up over a spectacular arrangement of dried flowers.

'Game, set and match to Mary Michaelmas!' said my grandmother.

The next day we were to go to the Christmas Fair—held these days at the end of November. I awoke to a morning of heavy frost, with a thick white mist hiding everything, and the sun a dull red eye peering at the strange, silent, hidden world. After breakfast I went out into the garden. The mist was thinning now as the sun shone through, and although the frost had blackened many of the flowers, the gold-edged ivy still brightened the old grey stone jars on the patio. A dead beech leaf stood up like a small brown sail, trapped in the ice on the pond. And everywhere there were frosted spiders' webs.

I helped to load various pots of preserves into boxes and then into the car, and we set off for the church hall. The village of Horwood lies in a countryside of gentle hills, broad fields and tall trees—though many of the trees had been uprooted in the October gales, and now lay like fallen giants, their roots heaving up into the air above the great holes torn in the ground. It was a long winding road, climbing all the way, and for most of the time we had it to ourselves. A squirrel darted across the road and climbed the bare branches of a walnut tree. We saw a magpie strutting in a ploughed field.

'That means bad luck,' said my grandmother. 'They say

"one for sorrow, two for joy"—though why anyone should think two magpies are better than one I can't think, they're nasty spiteful birds and they peck all my apples . . .'

I thought of the Magpie Inn, and Magpie Lane. I thought of Darius . . .

The hedgerows and verges were hung with the fine gossamer of spiders' webs, like bridal veils tossed carelessly over the tall grasses and stiff twigs.

We swung round the last corner and saw ahead of us the small grey church and the red brick hall beside it. The forecourt was full of vans and cars and bikes, but my grandmother spotted the one remaining parking space and slid the car neatly into it. I struggled out with a heavy box of preserves and carried it towards the hall. The low sun slanted across the forecourt and lit up a spider's web, trembling and glittering high up on the porch. And in one corner of the web, the remains of a fly tightly wrapped in its white shroud, reminding me that spiders' webs are not pretty bridal veils. They are very efficient death-traps.

I felt a little shiver run through me, and was glad to get into the cheerful bustle of the church hall.

There was plenty of time before the Fair would be officially opened, so I walked around looking at the stalls, and inevitably I found myself at the one with the second-hand books. It was depressing to see them all, many of them bestsellers in their day, now shabby and forlorn, their author's names quite forgotten. And then I saw it: *Modern Marrakech: A Notebook* by Darius Underwood!

I'd given up all hope of finding a copy. Indeed, I had almost begun to suspect that no such book existed. But here it was, and I bought it for ten pence.

The photograph on the dustjacket was worth more than that. Darius looked out at me gravely from a background of white-walled houses on a hot and dusty street.

My heart began doing flip-flaps.

'He's a nice-looking young man, that Mr Underwood,' said the stall-holder. 'I heard him give a talk to the Literary Society. That's when I bought the book . . .'

'Did you enjoy reading it?' I asked eagerly.

'Well, to be truthful,' she said, 'I didn't enjoy it nearly as much as his talk. But I expect *you'll* like it,' she added hurriedly, remembering that she had just sold it to me.

There was no time to read it. Father Christmas arrived accompanied by a troop of snowmen, angels and some enchanting little cherubs. They *wished* us a Merry Christmas, they *wished* us a Merry Christmas, they *wished* us a Merry Christmas and a Happy New Year. Then Father Christmas went off to Santa's Grotto, the snowmen and angels took up their posts behind the stalls, and the enchanting little cherubs fused all the fairy lights.

When my grandmother and I got home again, late in the afternoon, I left her to doze by the fire while I ran up to my room with the book. People who write books give themselves away on every page. What was I going to learn about Darius?

One thing at least I knew already. He had faced the blank paper in the typewriter, he had slaved over the construction of the narrative and the shaping of the paragraphs, crossing out sentences and re-jigging them, choosing his words with all the skill that he possessed, so that his readers could see Marrakech as he saw it. And now *I* was going to see Marrakech as he saw it.

I took a deep breath and opened the book.

My first morning in Marrakech! Having perused the somewhat antiquated news from England that was to be found in a week-old copy of *The Times*, I sallied forth to sample the delights of the ancient city . . .

I gaped.

I turned a few pages, hoping that the first one was a mistake.

I turned a few more pages, and more, and more—they were all written in the same vein.

The silly, supercilious, patronizing, lazy *idiot*!

I hurled the book across the room.

CHAPTER 7

ST VALENTINE'S DAY

January was a slack month for me as far as talks went, but February was another matter altogether. Luncheon and supper clubs and literary societies all over the country made the astonishing discovery that St Valentine's Day occurs in February, so what better subject could they have for their February meeting than a talk by a romantic novelist? If I accepted every invitation that came in I should have been booked solid every day and evening for the whole of February. The thought of all those meetings and meals gave me a kind of mental indigestion. There was also the little matter of *Trinket at my Wrist*, the new book that was just beginning to take shape and needed a lot of attention. My first commitment was to my writing and my readers, and if I didn't keep turning out my books I might find that I no longer had any readers—and if no readers, then no more bookings through the Crispin Speakers' Agency. So I reasoned with myself, and never once mentioned the fact that of all the miserable times of year to travel, February takes the soggy biscuit.

So I accepted the first few bookings that came along, including one for a luncheon club meeting which was actually on February 14th itself. The other invitations I declined with regret and a very pleasant sense of being well and truly run after.

Well, that was the idea. But then on the morning of February 14th I had a phone call from Julian Leigh.

'Astolat, darling girl,' he said, 'I'm in a terrible hole—Philippa's away, and I've just had a phone call to say one of our speakers has gone down with flu. I need someone to take her place. Could you do it?'

'When's it for?' I asked, reaching for my diary.

'Tonight,' said Julian.

'Oh no,' I said, putting the diary down firmly. 'I'm sorry, Julian, I can't. I've got a luncheon club engagement today at Stanton Waveley.'

'I know,' said Julian. 'That's why—I mean, that's one of the reasons that I thought of you. The evening booking is not all that far from Stanton Waveley. It's at a place called —wait a minute—Barrswood—on the main line to London, same as Stanton Waveley . . .'

'But, Julian, I'm starting work on a new book,' I said. 'I've planned to take all my notebooks with me and work on the train coming back from Stanton Waveley.'

'Darling Astolat, this is an *emergency*,' said Julian. 'Honestly, I wouldn't ask you otherwise. But you'd be the *perfect* person to do the job, because it's a St Valentine's Day engagement and they'd booked a romantic novelist.'

'Which one?' I said.

Julian took a deep breath.

'It's the Contessa della Stola,' he said.

'Is she being dried out *again*?' I asked.

'She's *supposed* to be suffering from influenza,' said Julian. He didn't sound entirely convinced about that.

The Contessa is said to have an extravagant lifestyle, far more interesting than anything that ever happened in any of her books.

'I'm not much of a substitute for the Contessa,' I said. 'They'll be expecting somebody terribly exciting.'

'They'll be expecting somebody *sober*,' said Julian drily. 'Somebody reliable and *professional*.'

Sober, reliable, professional. That was how Julian saw me. It was a pretty fair assessment, and a few months ago I should have prided myself on the description. Now I wasn't so sure . . .

'*Anything* is better than turning up to give a talk and falling flat on your face,' said Julian. 'The Contessa's nothing but a bloody *amateur* . . .'

I hesitated.

'*Darling* Astolat,' said Julian, 'for the honour of romantic novelists everywhere, you'll *have* to take her place.'

That was quite a good point. Like most romantic novelists, I seethe at the way so many people picture us as bird-brains living in cloud-cuckoo-land. Bird-brains don't turn out a couple of saleable novels every year, year after year—and a good many romantic novelists produce other books as well. But to have a popular romantic novelist turning up drunk—or not turning up at all—would not improve our image.

'Well,' I said, 'I suppose I *could* do it—but before I say yes, I'll have to check the trains.'

'I've got the timetable in front of me,' said Julian. 'What time do you reckon to finish at Stanton Waveley?'

'About three o'clock,' I said. 'I've planned to catch the three-thirty train to London from Stanton Waveley.'

'The three-thirty from Stanton Waveley,' said Julian, 'arrives at Barrswood at four-ten. Mrs Winters—that's the Barrswood secretary—could meet you at Barrswood Station, take you home, give you tea, get you to her meeting at seven-thirty—and afterwards she could take you to the station in time to catch the ten-four to London. You'll be in London just after eleven p.m.'

'I'll want a first-class ticket,' I said. 'I still want to do some work on my new book.'

'The Agency will pay the extra,' said Julian.

'I've still got to get home to Blackheath,' I said.

'Take a taxi,' said Julian grandly. 'Send me the bill and the Agency will reimburse you.'

It was a chance not to be missed. The Agency was not noted for its generosity.

'Well . . .' I said.

'I *knew* I could rely on you, darling,' said Julian. 'I'll telephone Mrs Winters and tell her to meet you this afternoon—four-ten at Barrswood. I'm *eternally* grateful to you, Astolat. You've absolutely *saved* the Agency. *Bless* you, dear heart . . .'

He rang off, and I began to collect my scattered wits and curse myself for an easy-going idiot. Then I looked at the clock and realized that I hadn't got time for such a luxury —I'd just about got time to pack my bag and head for Stanton Waveley.

It was a cold morning, but dry and sunny, and I wore the crimson velvet. I managed to get a first-class carriage all to myself, and did a lot of work on *Trinket at my Wrist*, so I was quite happy. The luncheon club engagement was pleasant but uneventful—in view of subsequent events, perhaps I should say that it was pleasant *and* uneventful.

I caught the three-thirty train from Stanton Waveley, and managed to do a good half-hour's work on my notebooks before I began to wonder if there would be anyone to meet me at Barrswood. If Philippa had been doing the organizing I should have had no worries—but Julian . . .

I stepped down from the train at Barrswood, and found a green Mercedes waiting for me. Either Julian was a better organizer than I had thought, or Philippa had returned to the office and had taken over.

'How do you do? I'm Enid Winters, Secretary of the Barrswood Literary Society . . .'

Mrs Winters was cool and cheerfully efficient. She took my bag, piloted me to the car, tucked me in, and drove me to her home for a cup of tea and a chance to relax in front of the fire.

'It's very good of you to come to our rescue,' she said. 'I have to admit I wasn't looking forward to an evening with Contessa What's-Her-Name—I've been dreading having to pronounce her name at the meeting.'

'Why don't you just refer to her as the Contessa?' I said.

'Well, of course, now that you're here, I can do that and then go on to introduce you—oh, by the way, how do you pronounce your name?'

'With the accent on the first syllable,' I said. 'It rhymes with "As to that" . . .'

We smiled at each other.

'This is my first season as Secretary,' said Mrs Winters. 'There's far more to this job than I realized when I took it on. But I'm gradually getting things organized the way I want them. We've got a marvellous Catering Committee to provide teas—I'm awfully keen on that, it's a chance for people to get together and have a chat.'

'Are all your speakers literary people?' I asked.

'Well, no,' she said. 'We've gone for *entertainment* rather than purely literary subjects. You see, Barrswood is quite a small place, and I don't think we'd be able to hold our membership if our meetings were devoted entirely to literature.'

'What sort of speakers do you have?' I asked.

'Well, our first speaker this season—that was the September meeting, of course, our season begins in September—she was an expert on indoor gardens. She's written a number of books about them, but she's not primarily a writer. She brought a lovely display of sink gardens and pot plants—that's one of hers over there.'

She indicated a miniature sink garden near the window.

'Did you buy it from her after the meeting?' I asked.

'Yes,' she said. 'She sold quite a lot of her display. Then

in October we had a very jolly woman who talked about music, and performed songs at the piano . . .'

'Who did you have in November?' I asked.

'November—oh yes, now that was decidedly literary,' she said. 'We had a poetry reading all about autumn— '*season of mists and mellow fruitfulness*' and all that. And in December we had a man who made candles—'

'Candles?' I said.

'Yes. Philippa Preston recommended him specially, and he was most interesting. He brought along moulds and waxes and coloured candles of all kinds. I remember he had Father Christmas candles and penguin candles—lots of us bought them for Christmas decorations.'

What excellent timing, I thought. Close enough to Christmas for people to be thinking of decorations, but a bit too close for them to have the time to make their own fancy candles. What a *sensible* woman Philippa Preston was!

'Oh, and he had one gorgeous candle, like a tall block of marble, all purple and orange swirls. He called it the Dream Tower. And he brought some red candles shaped like hearts —you'll see some of them at the party tonight.'

'Party?' I said, suddenly alert. 'Isn't it just a straightforward meeting?'

'Oh yes,' said Mrs Winters. 'At least, it is to begin with. We start with your talk, but then afterwards—that's after Question Time, of course—we're going to move into another room and have a St Valentine's Day party. Now I know you have to catch your train, and I don't want to delay you, but would you mind just cutting the cake for us?'

'Oh no,' I said. 'I—'

'It wouldn't take more than a few minutes,' she said, 'and I promise I'll get you to the station by ten o'clock in time for your train.'

'I'm an absolute novice at cake-cutting,' I said, terrified

at the thought of ruining the Catering Committee's centre-piece. 'I'd make a terrible mess—'

'Oh, the cake's cut already,' said Mrs Winters. 'Or at least it will be by the time the meeting begins. It's really just an excuse to take some photographs of you posed in front of the buffet with the members of the Society around you. Some of our members are enthusiastic photographers and they'll all want to take pictures of you—especially when they see you in that crimson velvet . . . Oh please, Miss Astolat, it would be such a marvellous exercise in audience participation.'

'If we finish the first part of the evening in time, OK,' I said. 'But if for any reason we over-run, then I'm afraid I'd have to go straight to the station. I can keep my talk short —but I'd have to rely on you to keep Question Time on a tight rein.'

'Can do,' said Mrs Winters. 'I wonder, would you like me to send you a set of photographs when they're ready? Well now, I think it's almost time for us to be off to the Community Centre . . .'

Barrswood Community Centre was a pleasant, modern building, not at all handsome, but warm and brightly lit, and—judging by the posters on the notice-board—fulfilling its duties to the community by providing a home for children's disco-dancing classes, jumble sales, aerobics, concerts and back-pain sufferers.

Our meeting was held in the main hall. When we arrived the ceremony of arranging the chairs was in full swing, and I could hear cups and saucers rattling behind the shuttered serving-hatch. A thin, elderly lady wearing a grey and white dress and looking rather like a heron waiting to pounce sat at a table just inside the entrance, ready to take entrance money. The hall soon filled up, and there were only a few empty seats at seven-thirty when the meeting began.

Mrs Winters introduced me to the audience.

'I'm sorry to have to tell you that the Contessa dell—
er—' her courage failed her—'the Contessa is indisposed
and can't be with us this evening—'

There was some whispering and murmuring—several
members of the audience were disappointed.

'—but I'm very pleased to be able to tell you that we
have a most distinguished writer in her place—and at only
a few hours' notice . . . Here to talk to us about *Romantic
Novelists Today*—just the subject for a meeting on St Valentine's Day—Miss Elaine Astolat.'

There was even more murmuring, and an outbreak of
applause. I was glad to realize that a lot of people in the
audience had the good sense to be pleased at the change of
speaker. I went into my act, and all was going well when
there was the sound of a bus stopping noisily just outside
the Community Centre. Doors slammed, and half a dozen
people came tumbling into the hall.

'So sorry, Contessa,' called one of the late-comers. 'But
the bus was late . . .'

Everybody shushed her, and I waited while the late-
comers paid at the door and slid into the seats that had
been kept for them by their friends. I noticed that there
were two men who didn't seem to have any friends. One
was a plump, pasty-faced man in a raincoat who tiptoed
forward and sat at the end of the front row. The other one
found a seat near the back. He was a small, thin man with
a narrow mouth, protruding teeth and a rather pink nose
that twitched every few minutes. I thought of him as the
Rabbit, and wished he wouldn't twitch quite so often.

For my reading at the end of the talk I had chosen some
passages from a book which had not been selling as well as
expected, and when it came to Question Time the man in
the raincoat asked me for its name.

'It's called *Dreams and Shadows*,' I said, glad of the chance
to plug it.

'It sounded very nice,' he said. 'I'd like to buy a copy for the wife. I'm sure she'd like it.'

'That's very kind of you,' I said. 'You can get it at any bookshop.'

He looked disappointed, but before he could say any more Mrs Winters, mindful of her promise, brought the meeting smartly to a close, and soon afterwards led me into a side room where the Catering Committee had laid out a magnificent buffet for St Valentine's Day.

As Mrs Winters had promised, there were heart-shaped candles. There were also heart-shaped cakes, heart-shaped sandwiches and heart-shaped quiches. The centrepiece was a large iced cake topped by a red satin heart. This was the cake that I was to pretend to cut for the benefit of the photographers.

There was an ornate cake-knife for me to use, almost as big as a ceremonial sword. I tried holding it in different ways, and made a few practice stabs to get the feel of it. People began drifting in. The photographers came in, bubbling with excitement and brandishing cameras of all kinds and producing a jumble of camera cases, light meters, flashcubes and a great deal of a technical chat. Mrs Winters herded them together at one end of the room. Only one photographer kept aloof—the old grey heron lady. She had an elderly Leica, and she was sitting down quietly and looking on. I thought that perhaps she was too old for standing about, or perhaps she just knew from experience what a long time some of the other photographers took to get ready. I got into position and stood with the knife poised somewhere above the satin heart. Various members of the Society arrived and grouped themselves around me, the Catering Committee supplied them all with glasses of red wine, and then we waited for the photographers.

It was at this moment that the man in the raincoat slid to my side.

'Could I buy that book—you know, the one about the dreams?' he said.

'Of course,' I said. 'You can get it at any bookshop.'

The minutes were ticking by. I didn't want to hold up the photographers when they were ready, if they ever were. Even more, I didn't want to miss my train back to London.

'No,' he said. 'I mean—the copy you have with you. I don't mind paying a bit extra for it . . .'

'I'm sorry,' I said. 'I've already promised it to a friend.' (This was untrue, but I hate selling my books at meetings. And I had a train to catch.)

A single camera clicked.

'Smile, please,' said the cameraman. 'Everybody raise your glasses . . .'

'Oh, sorry, I'm in the way,' said the man in the raincoat. 'Don't want to spoil the picture . . .'

He backed away and disappeared.

Several flashes went off, and everybody jumped, including me.

I made several pretend cuts in the cake, and the flash cubes went off again. Then the Secretary's husband Colin lifted the satin heart off the cake, went down on one knee and presented it to me with a fine flourish. The photographers asked him to do it again. And again . . . At last they were satisfied. Mrs Winters helped me on with my coat. I dropped the red satin heart into my overnight bag.

'Hey!' cried Colin Winters in mock alarm. 'Be careful with my heart!'

'Don't worry, I'll take good care of it,' I said, laughing. I patted my bag. 'I've got all my valuables in here—so your heart's in good company.'

'One moment . . . souvenir . . .'

A photographer with a Polaroid camera dashed up to me, waving a just-developed picture. It showed me talking to the man in the raincoat—not perhaps the picture I would have chosen as a souvenir.

'Thanks very much,' I said. 'I'm sorry, but I have to fly now . . .'

I waved the photograph in the air so that everyone could see it, dropped it into my overnight bag and departed in a flurry of farewells. The Rabbit held the door open for me. I noticed a long strip of sticking-plaster across his knuckles.

Poor little Rabbit, I thought. I can see you're the accident-prone type. And I gave him a specially warm smile as I went past.

Mrs Winters swept me off in the green Mercedes. As we drove down the slope to the station forecourt we saw a man in a raincoat hurrying into the ticket office, and when we got on to the platform there was the pasty-faced man waiting for us.

'We meet again,' he said, and smiled.

Mrs Winters smiled back, desperately trying to recall his name.

'Oh, hallo, Mr—Um,' she said at last.

'May I help you with your bag?' he said, and before I could stop her, she handed him my overnight bag. I could hardly grab it back, but it contained my notes for *Trinket at my Wrist*, and I would have preferred to keep hold of it myself. I cursed Mrs Winters and Mr Um. The train arrived, and Mr Um helped me into the crowded carriage, steered me into a gangway seat and put my bag into the space behind me.

Just before the train started, a man jumped down the steps of the footbridge, landed as neatly as a gymnast, and sprinted past our window. He looked remarkably like the Rabbit. But it couldn't have been him. That had been quite a jump, and the accident-prone Rabbit would have landed in a heap and probably broken his ankle into the bargain.

I saw Mrs Winters standing on the platform, ready to

wave us goodbye. She was smiling, but for me the happiness of the St Valentine's Day party was evaporating.

The train started with a jerk that sent several late-comers staggering backwards, clutching at each other for support and sitting down sooner than expected.

I was cross with Mr Um. He had shepherded me into a second-class carriage when I had a perfectly good first-class ticket, and he had put my white overnight bag into the space behind my seat so that I couldn't keep my eye on it. I knew that I was being unfair, and that the person I was really cross with was myself. I ought to have thanked Mr Um for his help, and then taken my bag and gone off to find myself a first-class carriage where I could settle down and do some work on my new book. But I couldn't do it. The poor man looked so pleased to be of service.

He sat down opposite me and smiled shyly. There was a table between us, and our neighbours in the window seats had cans of lager and the remains of two packets of sandwiches in front of them.

Two girls with punk hairdo's came flying into the carriage with cups of coffee, leaving the sliding door open behind them. The man sitting next to the door protested, but they shouted obscenities at him as they continued down the carriage past us and out at the door behind me.

Mr Um apologized to me for their behaviour. Then he tugged at his raincoat pocket.

'May I ask you—as a very great favour—to have a look at this for me?'

I knew what was coming. A manuscript.

I was absolutely furious. He had scraped acquaintance with me, and now he was taking advantage of it.

'I'm afraid I don't read manuscripts,' I said coldly.

He thrust a sheaf of scrappy, hand-written pages across the table towards me.

'Oh, please, just have a look at it . . . it would mean so much to me . . .'

I glanced at it.

'First of all,' I said severely, 'you'll have to get your work typed professionally . . .'

'Typed?' he said. 'Oh, but I couldn't do that . . . I mean, I couldn't ask any of the young ladies in the typing pool to type something like *this*.'

I knew then what kind of manuscript it was going to be. I read the opening sentence.

He ripped open her dress to the waist, and stared greedily at her round white breasts as they heaved with passion. A hot surge of lust went through him and he seized her in his arms and brought his mouth down upon her tight pink nipples.

I looked up. He was watching me intently. There was an unpleasant sense of excitement about him. Was he hoping that I was going to tell him that he'd written a masterpiece? Or was he just hoping to embarrass me and getting a nasty little thrill out of it?

The two punk girls tore back through the carriage, knocking newspapers and books to the floor as they passed, leaving the sliding door open again. The patient man by the door closed it behind them.

I adopted my best schoolmistress manner.

'If you don't like the idea of having your work typed by anybody else,' I said, 'then you will have to type it yourself. No publisher would look at such a badly written manuscript.'

'Oh, but just look at this bit,' he said. He leaned across the table and pointed a stubby finger at the bottom of the page. I sighed and looked down, and as I did so, I caught a glimpse of a hand removing my white bag from behind my seat, a hand with a strip of sticking-plaster across the knuckles.

The Rabbit!

He hurried past me down the gangway.

I jumped to my feet.

'Here!' said Mr Um, hurt at my lack of interest in his bodice-ripper.

'He's got my bag!' I cried, and started in pursuit.

I ran down the gangway and through the sliding door, and I could hear Mr Um running after me. As I ran into the next carriage I could see the two punk girls coming towards me carrying more supplies from the buffet car. They took one look at my face and cowered out of my way —a tigress with cubs to defend has nothing on a writer in defence of her latest work.

The Rabbit streaked through the next carriage, but I was gaining on him. Behind me I could hear Mr Um puffing and panting as he pounded gamely after me.

We came to the guard's van. The big cage was empty save for something that looked and sounded like the Hound of the Baskervilles leaping about and tugging at a heavy chain.

I was still gaining on the Rabbit when Mr Um gave a sudden lurch and bumped into me, knocking me against the wall of the van.

'Sorry—lost my balance,' he gasped.

The idiot had put me off my stride, and I had lost the advantage I had been gaining.

I saw the Rabbit run through the next carriage. Beyond him was the crowded buffet car. That should slow him down, I thought viciously. Slow him down! Of course, *that* was what I should have done in the first place! Slow *everything* down!

With great deliberation I reached up and pulled the communication cord.

It was a lovely feeling.

'You've done it, now, Contessa!' said Mr Um.

I turned to him, surprised.

'I'm not the Contessa,' I said.

His mouth fell open. He made one or two unsuccessful attempts to speak.

'Gawd!' he croaked at last. 'I'll . . . I'll fetch the guard!'

He turned and started lumbering away towards the rear of the train.

'Tell him to get the police!' I shouted.

I could feel the train beginning to slow down, as though it was approaching a station. I ran through the next carriage. Ahead of me, the Rabbit was having a job to force his way through the crowd in the buffet car. I'd be glad to have Mr Um and the guard behind me in case of trouble.

The train was definitely slowing down, but nobody else seemed to notice. I steadied myself on seat-backs as I went by. Ahead of me the buffet car was packed solid with people. The train had started with a bit of a jerk; it might also stop with one.

It did.

I had just reached the entrance to the buffet car when a shudder seemed to pass along the whole length of the train. There was a loud clanking sound as the carriages came to a halt. And suddenly I had a clear view right through the buffet car as everybody there fell over.

I had a glimpse of the Rabbit hurtling through the carriage beyond the buffet car, and then he disappeared.

It was dark on the floor of the car, and uproar broke out as the buffet customers found their tongues. They were piled all over the place, sitting on each other's heads, draped over each other's feet, squirming and clutching at each other, each man blaming his neighbour for the catastrophe which had suddenly overtaken them. Lager and coffee spilled out in all directions, microwaved burgers were sat upon and crisps were trodden underfoot.

Beyond them I could see the guard walking through the train towards me. He stopped at the place where the Rabbit had disappeared. Then he too disappeared, and I expected him to reappear holding his captive, and my bag. But there was a long pause, and nothing seemed to be happening.

I began trying to pick my way over the heaving mass on the floor of the buffet car. Hands reached up and grabbed at me, feet kicked out at me, lager cans rolled about spilling their contents. But at last I was through, and hurrying to meet the guard, who was coming towards me, empty-handed.

For a moment I felt sorry for Mr Um, galloping all the way to the rear of the train when the guard had been at the front all the time. Then I grasped the significance of the guard's empty hands. Somehow the Rabbit had managed to escape with my bag.

'He's stolen my bag!' I shouted, waving to the guard to make him understand that he had gone right past the thief.

'Did you stop this train, madam?' asked the guard.

'He stole my bag!' I shouted again.

A voice from the floor shouted, 'It's under your arm, you silly cow!'

'This is my *hand*bag,' I said. 'The bag that was stolen was a white overnight bag.'

There was a good deal of profanity as the customers in the buffet car slowly righted themselves, and the guard thoughtfully drew me to one side and closed the sliding doors behind us. It was suddenly very quiet. I was conscious that in the usual English manner, everybody in the carriage was observing me, while giving the impression that they were engrossed in novels and newspapers.

'Now, madam, you say somebody has stolen your bag. Can you describe him to me?'

'He's small and thin,' I said. 'And he looks like a rabbit. His nose twitches all the time. And—and he's got a strip of sticking-plaster over his knuckles.'

There was a sudden, new commotion at the far end of the carriage. The sliding door opened and a big, burly man came into the carriage. I noticed two things immediately.

(a) he was carrying my white bag, and (b) his zipper was open. Everybody else noticed (b) first.

'There it is!' I cried.

The guard went towards the burly man and spoke quietly to him.

The man let out a roar.

'Of course it's not my bag!' he shouted. His voice was thick and blurry, and so was his vocabulary.

'Blurry bag in the blurry toilet—I couldn't open the blurry door . . .'

The guard took the bag from him, and the burly man went back the way he had come. A moment later the ENGAGED sign was illuminated above the carriage door.

The guard returned with the bag in his hand.

'Thank you so much!' I said breathlessly, and put out my hand to take the bag.

'Just a minute, madam,' said the guard. 'Can you identify the contents of this bag?'

I told myself that the man was only doing his job, only trying to help.

'It should contain one large red notepad with lots of shorthand notes,' I said. 'Also a small green notepad with more shorthand, and a black loose-leaf book. A blue toilet bag and matching hand-towel. A spare pair of tights. A torch. A paperback book. Oh yes, and a red satin heart— it was given to me this evening at a St Valentine's Day party.'

I had a feeling that there was something else, but I couldn't think what it was.

He took out the various items one by one and placed them on the seat. Everybody in the carriage craned to get a look.

'Can't see the book, madam,' he said. 'Everything else is here all right. Are you sure you packed the book?'

He looked at me very hard as he said that. I got the impression that if I made a fuss about *Dreams and Shadows* I should have to go through some official channels to get the bag back, whereas if I cut my losses . . .

'Well,' I said, 'I suppose I *could* have dropped the book somewhere. And anyway, I can easily replace it.' (Only too easily, I thought, remembering its sales record.)

The guard smiled. I had said the right thing. No need for official reports and inquiries and Transport Police and other time-consuming matters.

He gave the bag back to me.

'Oh, thank you!' I cried. 'You don't know how much this means to me . . .'

There was a little gleam in his eye, which showed that he might be interested to find out, so I gave him the largest note in my wallet. I'd have paid far more than that to get my notebooks back. He smiled.

'For your information, madam, it looks as though the thief shoved your bag just inside the door of the toilet and then jumped down on to the track when the train stopped. The carriage door was left open, but I made a thorough investigation and ascertained that there is no sign of any-body (did he mean "anybody" or "any body"?) down there, so he must have got away in the darkness. I'll inform the driver that he can resume the journey . . .'

He departed.

Poor little Rabbit! He was accident-prone in more ways than one. He must have hoped for quite a haul. If he'd had time to look inside the bag he'd have been terribly disappointed. I remembered calling out to Colin Winters, 'I've got all my valuables in here . . .' It would never have occurred to the Rabbit that I was referring to my notebooks.

I picked them up and smoothed them lovingly before replacing them in the bag. I put back the toilet bag, and the towel, and the torch, and the spare pair of tights. I felt the eyes of the other passengers upon me. I couldn't disappoint them. Smiling, I picked up the red satin heart and held it up for everyone to see. Twelve pairs of eyes dropped at once to their respective novels and newspapers.

I tucked the heart inside the bag and turned towards the buffet car, and as I did so, I felt a slight shudder run through the train. The driver was about to start.

With another jerk?

Yes.

I braced myself against the shock, but the customers in the buffet car did not. When the jolt came, they teetered on the lager-wet floor, clutching each other for support.

I didn't wait. I stepped over and round and I fear upon some of them, and fled through the train.

As I ran through the guard's van, the Hound of the Baskervilles gave tongue, but I didn't stop. I wanted to get back to my seat—and, with a slight pang of remorse at having forgotten all about him—I wanted to tell Mr Um that everything was all right.

But I was too late.

Of Mr Um and his grubby manuscript there was no sign.

Perhaps my cry of 'Get the police!' had alarmed him. However much he might have enjoyed watching me read his manuscript, he might not relish the thought of the police reading it. And it wouldn't exactly enhance his standing in the Barrswood Literary Society.

CHAPTER 8

BRAVE NEW WORLD

By now I had become quite an old hand at travelling up and down the country addressing groups of all kinds, in places ranging from small huts lit by gas and with windows streaming with condensation to overheated dining-rooms in very expensive hotels.

Despite my adventure on St Valentine's Day, I always

travelled by train. On a train I could write up my notes, correct my proofs and work on a new book, none of which would be possible if I were driving a car. And of course sometimes I overheard conversations which might spark off ideas for another story. There is yet another advantage about travelling by train—there is very little scope for Treasurers to argue over expenses when they are presented with a train ticket. Mileage expenses for car travel sometimes invite a spot of haggling, or so I have been told.

By now, of course, I had learned the importance of getting my expenses paid before I left an engagement, and I had learned how to open envelopes and check cheques without looking too mercenary.

I had learned to stifle my screams when anybody said, 'I've always thought I'd like to write, but I've never had the time.'

I had also learned, to my embarrassment, that some people read things into my books that I would never dream of writing.

I had learned to send publicity material to the Club Secretaries two months before an engagement, so that they could plug me as a forthcoming attraction. Some Secretaries would send advance notices to the local press and follow with a brief write-up, and some very nice Secretaries sent me copies of the resulting press cuttings, although their well-meant efforts were frequently undermined by the printers. I remember that one chivalrous Secretary referred to me as 'the delectable Miss Astolat', but according to the printers Elaine Astolat was merely 'deletable'. The title of my novel, *The Queen's Red Rose*, came out as *The Queen's Red Nose*, while *My Dear Cath* became *My Dead Cat*.

But of course all the time the person who was going on these expeditions wasn't *me* at all. It was a completely fictitious character who wore 'romantic' clothes because that was what her audiences expected, who was accustomed to being the centre of attention, who walked confidently into meetings and knew that she would be welcomed and applauded. The whole thing was utterly false. The real me was always tucked away safely in the Lady of Shalott's tower, watching the pretend Astolat going through her routine. I had to admit that it was fun, but I was always half-afraid that somebody would unmask me as a fraud, and there were times when I had a sneaking feeling that if I looked into a mirror I should see a doppelganger grinning over my shoulder.

Late in July I had an evening engagement to address a Ladies' Supper Club which would involve an overnight stay at a place called King's Martlet. A few days beforehand I began looking up maps and train timetables, and found that the nearest station was Bettesham. The name sounded familiar but I couldn't place it. Then I recalled Philippa saying she had worked at the Bettesham Repertory Theatre when Julian and Mary were the stars there. And somebody else had mentioned Bettesham . . .

I looked through the papers in my file and a pink booklet fell out. As I stooped to pick it up I saw the message in large letters:

DO NOT ALLOW THIS BOOK TO BE READ BY
ANY OF OUR SPEAKERS

Then, in smaller letters at the very top, written in blue ink:

Mrs Bunty Beresford, King's Martlet Ladies' Supper Club, near Bettesham.

Memory came flooding back.

The Royal Casterbridge Hotel . . .

Darius Underwood . . .

The Fretful Porpentine with the hedgehog hat . . .

Bunty Beresford lying dead . . .

and

RED FOR DANGER.

CHAPTER 9

KING'S MARTLET

It was glorious summer weather, and I wore my floaty pink dress with the crystal-pleated sleeves the afternoon that I took the train to Bettesham. A youth with a vacant expression was drinking himself glassy-eyed with a succession of miniature brandies. There were few other people in the carriage, and they were well spread out, keeping themselves to themselves in true English fashion, each one occupying a seat designed for two, and in some cases, a pair of seats designed for four, by the simple expedient of spreading their belongings around and glaring at any newcomers until they drifted off and found similar space for themselves.

I was working out ideas for a new book. Everything was still at the amorphous stage when nothing was fixed and even the characters hadn't made up their minds what they were going to look like or how they were going to talk, so I sat back and looked idly out of the window while my subconscious mind acted as a sorting-office for ideas. I watched the countryside speeding by—pastureland green and softly swelling, dotted with sheep and cows, and arable land with grain almost ripe for harvest.

After a while I began to notice how very attractive some of the smaller stations had become. Where once they had been a uniform porridge-and-pine-green, now their Victorian ironwork was painted in pale green or ivory or mauve or pillar-box red—their brickwork had been cleaned up to display the coloured patterns built into the walls and around the windows—some of them even had hanging flower-baskets.

Shortly before we were due to arrive at Bettesham we

stopped at one of these little stations. The iron columns supporting the framework of the roof were painted a demurely respectable matt black, but around them twined a seductive spiral of ribbons picked out in pale gold. Half way up each column came a ring of gilded cloverleaves, and the top was encircled by a ring of daffodils, each leaf and stem a brilliant green, each flower a golden trumpet. It was impossible to look at them and not feel a spark of pleasure that somebody had recognized the potential of columns that in other stations had their ribbons and flowers hidden under a thick coating of shiny black treacle.

I made a rough sketch in my notebook. The station might provide a setting for a story some time.

I was still sketching when the bleary-eyed youth got up, took his bag from the luggage rack and headed for one of the toilets. We must be getting near Bettesham. Everybody began to gather their scattered belongings together. When the bleary-eyed one returned, he was transformed. He now sported an extraordinary costume of white T-shirt and shorts and a long shiny scarlet cape. The T-shirt bore the legend B F in scarlet lettering.

The other passengers had kept a furtive eye on the amount of brandy he was drinking, but they had been brought up on the idea that it was rude to stare, and they now averted their eyes from him. So I was the only person to look at him at all closely, and probably the only person to realize that his T-shirt was advertising the Bettesham Festival, but that for some reason only the two big capital letters had been printed in red. The remaining letters were printed in white on the white ground of his T-shirt and were to all intents and purposes invisible. He had my sympathy. If I'd had to wear that outfit in public I too might have required a few brandies.

As the train drew in to Bettesham I saw a swarm of white balloons bobbing about over the footbridge, and as the train stopped, the balloons were carried down the steps on to the platform by a horde of excited girls and boys, dressed like the youth, but without his scarlet cape. Every T-shirt and every white balloon was emblazoned with the two scarlet letters, and they all surged towards our carriage door. There was a shrill cheer as our fellow-traveller stepped down on to the platform. For a moment he was engulfed, and then he was escorted in triumph up the steps and over the footbridge.

I followed at a discreet distance and came out into the sunny forecourt where cameras were waiting. There was also an organizer, a woman who had reached years of discretion, although despite this she wore the standard BF outfit. She marshalled her troops in front of the station's only exit and began handing out Olympic-style flaring torches to the youth and some of the older children. They held them aloft like so many Statues of Liberty. The photographers fell upon their knees and took pictures.

A wedge of irritated passengers trying to leave the station now built up behind the group. There was a similar build-up of cars and taxis trying to get into the station forecourt, since the Organizer had parked her minibus smack across the entrance. A couple of taxi-drivers advanced to point out her error.

'That's for the opening of the Bettesham Festival, you know,' said a woman standing beside me. 'They're going to run all through Bettesham and then up the hill to the race-course, and then they're going to light a bonfire with their torches.'

'Sounds fun,' I said weakly.

'That's my Charlene standing next to that Hank—that's what they call him, Hank—No, I don't know who he is— he's not a pop star, that I do know, because my Charlene's got all their pictures in her room. I've never seen him before. I think he must be a sportsman . . .'

I agreed. If Hank was going to run through Bettesham in that costume with that bunch of kids, and then run uphill to the race-course, he was undoubtedly a sportsman.

The taxi-drivers had convinced the Organizer that it was time for her to get the show on the road. The group was moved away from the station entrance, and the bottled-up passengers surged out. The minibus was moved from the forecourt entrance, and the bottled-up cars and taxis surged in.

I couldn't bear to look, so I turned away and surveyed the posters on the wall behind me. Two familiar faces caught my eye—two large heads of Julian Leigh and Mary Michaelmas, surrounded by smaller photographs in oval frames showing them as Romeo and Juliet, as Hamlet and Ophelia, as Antony and Cleopatra. The poster informed me that Julian and Mary were to perform *A Lover and his Lass* in the Great Hall of Bettesham Court as part of the Bettesham Festival. The price of the tickets included wine and light refreshments, as well it might.

I thought of the last time I had seen those photographs, spread out on the glass-topped table at Crispin Wharf House, when I had behaved so badly to Julian, and Julian had behaved so badly to me, and Darius had come to my rescue and walked me along Magpie Lane. I wondered where Darius was now . . .

'Miss AsTOHlat?' said a voice. 'I'm Jenny Robbins of the Ladies' Supper Club.'

I turned, and saw a pleasant middle-aged woman smiling at me.

'Hallo, Mrs Robbins,' I said. 'Yes, I'm Elaine Astolat.'

'Oh, there now, did I pronounce your name wrong? I'm sorry about that,' she said. 'And I'm sorry you've had to stand about waiting, but there was quite a traffic hold-up —they said that was something to do with the opening of the Festival . . .'

She led me to her car and opened the door.

'Just a minute, Miss Astolat, let me put the rug over the seat—don't want to spoil your dress—Belinda's been moulting again . . . Careful with those sleeves . . . aren't they pretty? Anyone can tell you're a romantic writer . . .'

We drove through the wide tree-lined streets of Bettesham: rows of Regency terrace houses, all white paint and window-boxes, all doing bed-and-breakfasts; then along past the municipal gardens, the municipal offices and the solid Edwardian bulk of the Town Hall.

We negotiated a complicated system of one-way streets, and then found ourselves on the outskirts and starting to climb the hill towards the race-course.

'That's where they're going to open the Festival,' said Mrs Robbins. 'Pop groups, and a bonfire, and then fireworks.'

I wondered if this would affect the numbers attending the Ladies' Supper Club. Mrs Robbins must have read my thoughts.

'I don't think that will stop our ladies coming to hear you,' she said. 'They hear more than enough pop groups, and we get plenty of bonfires round here in the autumn . . .'

We were driving through winding country roads, where the hedges were starred with pink dog-roses. A few houses were dotted about, set well back from the road, and with fields all around them. Then we came to a huddle of black and white cottages, and we were in King's Martlet. It had a honey-coloured church, a cheerful red brick pub, and a small High Street whose shops and houses leaned together like old friends gossiping. As we turned up by the War Memorial, the early evening sunlight slanted across a low rambling house of faded red brick. It had white-framed windows and a gabled porch, and a few plum-trees casting long shadows over the grass.

'What a lovely old house!' I said.

Mrs Robbins obligingly slowed down so that I could see it better.

'That's where you'll be staying tonight,' she said. 'That used to belong to our late President, Bunty Beresford . . .'

It was easy to imagine Bunty living in a house like that,

presiding gracefully over the tea-table in her blue suit with the lace blouse.

'Her sister-in-law Mrs Gadsden owns it now. She's our new President . . . and she'll be your hostess for the night. The President always offers overnight hospitality to our speakers.'

'I believe I met Mrs Beresford once,' I said. 'She was a charming lady—I seem to remember she wore a lovely cameo brooch of the Three Graces . . .'

'Fancy you remembering that!' said Mrs Robbins. 'Yes, that was Bunty all right. She was a dear, and we all miss her very much. Perhaps I shouldn't say this, but her sister-in-law isn't a patch on her—not a patch. Bunty left the house to her in her will—they'd been living there together for years—*and* she left her whatever money she had, though between you and me there wasn't much of *that* . . .'

Mrs Robbins was a jewel. She was an efficient Secretary, she was a good driver, and best of all, she was a trifle indiscreet.

'Bunty was a lovely President,' she said. 'You see, Bunty was—well, she was a *lady* . . .'

Bunty's sister-in-law, I gathered, was not.

'I'm afraid Mrs Gadsden is just a little bit *pushy*,' said Mrs Robbins. 'You may find her a bit overbearing . . . oh dear, perhaps I shouldn't say that. She means well, and of course she *is* our President now. By the way, please don't mention Bunty to any of our members. Some of them are still very upset about her death, even though it happened over a year ago. Ah, here we are . . .'

She swung the car off the road and through a gateway with a signboard reading 'King's Martlet Country Club'. We drove along a winding carriageway, past manicured lawns set with cedars and cypresses, and stopped in front of a handsome old house of pale Cotswold stone, its classical lines softened by a number of hanging baskets filled with flowers and trails of ivy. Here Mrs Robbins parked the car, picked up my overnight bag and led me up a flight of steps to the Club.

I could hear discreet sounds coming from the kitchen, and rather less discreet sounds coming from the bar, and then I was plunged into a mass of strangers. Mrs Robbins, like an experienced sheepdog, cut one out of the flock and led her towards me, smiling.

'Miss AsTOH—I'm sorry, I mean Miss AStolat,' she said. 'Our President, Mrs Verena Gadsden.'

I saw a woman of imposing build, head poking forward and a dowager's hump. Brassy hair, a hard pencil line where her eyebrows should have been, and unbelievably white teeth. All that was missing was the hat like a hedgehog. I was face to face with Verena, the Fretful Porpentine of the Royal Casterbridge reception.

She didn't recognize me, of course. Why should she? The last time we met, I was a timid mouselike creature, one of a crowd. Now I was the centre of attention, the successful romantic writer in an appropriately romantic dress.

Verena Gadsden dismissed Mrs Robbins with a brusque nod, took me over, and introduced me to various members of the Supper Club. She piloted me to the cool, classical supper room, its pale green walls topped with white swags of plaster fruit and flowers. Three tall windows gave on to the lawns. Soft lights fell upon snowy tablecloths and sparkling crystal, and my floaty pink dress was in its element. It would have made a perfect setting for Bunty Beresford. But Verena did not fit in with her surroundings. She was abrupt in her remarks to the guests, and downright rude to the waitress who served us. And of course she didn't exactly endear herself to me when she informed me that she had often thought of writing but had never had the time . . .

At the end of the meal the waitresses closed the green curtains across the tall windows. Verena made short work of introducing me, and sat back. I rose to my feet.

'Madam President, and ladies—it-gives-me-great-pleasure-to-be-with-you-this-evening . . .' I was off. Talking. Reading from my latest book, *Sweet Dreams of Arcady*. Answering questions—all the usual ones. Then the Vote of Thanks. Embarrassed Treasurer thrusting envelope into my hand. Quick peek at cheque. Everything in order. End of meeting.

Mrs Robbins drove us both home to Verena's house, and left us at the gate.

'Good night, Verena, good night Miss Astolat . . .'

'Good night, Mrs Robbins,' I said.

Verena Gadsden said nothing, but busied herself unlocking the front door. I had a glimpse of a pleasantly old-fashioned living-room, and then I was whisked upstairs to a bedroom with sprigged wallpaper and pleasantly old-fashioned furniture. I felt sure that this had once been Bunty's own room.

'Breakfast at eight o'clock do you?' said Verena, and without waiting for an answer, added 'Bathroom's opposite.' And clumping downstairs she began switching off the lights and locking up.

I investigated the bathroom. It was old-fashioned, but it was not pleasant. A cast-iron bath that had seen better days, wall-tiles that were cracked and crazed, lino that was frankly scruffy.

I retired to my room with the sprigged wallpaper, switched off the light and opened the window. The sweetness of night-scented stocks drifted up in the warm air. Pale moths flickered about in the darkness, and some sleepy birds called to each other, and then fell silent. I climbed into bed and slept.

At eight o'clock the next morning I was downstairs in the living-room—no longer in my rose-pink outfit but wearing a cool summer dress. Sunlight came streaming in through the windows, lighting up the bow-fronted china cabinet with its Chelsea and Coalport, but also showing up the worn patches on the chintz-covered chairs and the faded green carpet.

In one corner of the room a large copper pedestal supported a Chinese bowl filled with dried flower petals. I stirred the petals tentatively to release their perfume, and almost at once I heard Bunty Beresford saying, 'Even my pot-pourri doesn't smell as nice as it used to . . .'

I sniffed. I'm no expert, but I've often helped Grandmother make her pot-pourri, and I could identify the various herbs and flowers that had gone into the filling of Bunty's Chinese bowl. Rose petals, lavender, jasmine, honeysuckle, rosemary, mint, lemon, cloves, orange . . . and something else, somewhere, that did not belong. For a split-second I had another, more elusive, memory that belonged farther back in the past than Bunty. But before I could track it down, Verena Gadsden came in. She was wearing a striped shirt over stone-coloured pants, and she swept me out to the kitchen, where the smell of fresh coffee banished the scent of pot-pourri.

The kitchen was astonishing. It was enormous, it was gleaming, and it was very, very new. Sunshine poured in through picture windows and lit up the red quarry tiles on the floor, the red cedarwood cupboards, the acres of shiny working surfaces, and the hood of beaten copper over the cooker. It glowed through a block of marble, all gold and purple swirls, that stood beside a pot plant on the windowsill.

'What a lovely kitchen,' I said.

Verena smiled.

'My dream kitchen,' she said, producing plates of bacon and eggs and hot rolls. 'I've always wanted it, and now I've got it. Plenty of other jobs to be done around the place, but they've had to wait. First things first, that's my motto. Lots of other houses round here have pretty good kitchens, but they can't hold a candle to this one . . .'

The word 'candle' rang a faint bell. I looked again at the block of marble. 'All orange and purple swirls,' Mrs Winters had said.

'Isn't that the Dream Tower?' I said, nodding towards the block of marble which wasn't marble but a candle.

'So you know about the Dream Tower?' said Verena.

She looked at me thoughtfully, and then changed the subject.

'Do you by any chance know the Contessa della Stola?' she asked.

'I've read some of her books,' I said, 'but I've never actually met her . . .'

The sight of the Dream Tower reminded me of the St Valentine's Day meeting at Barrswood.

'Oh yes—and I have deputized for her,' I said.

'Ah!' said Verena. '*Have* you now?'

She seemed quite impressed. Perhaps she felt that deputizing for a Contessa had somehow conferred a patent of nobility upon me. I dare say I had just as much claim to one as the Contessa—or just as little.

'Coffee?' said Verena.

'Please,' I said.

As she gave me the cup she said, 'I think perhaps I owe you an apology, Miss Astolat. I'll be frank with you: when the committee agreed to invite a romantic novelist to talk to us I particularly asked Mrs Robbins to book the Stola woman. But she misread my note and booked—'

'—the Astolat woman?' I said.

'That's right,' she said. 'I suppose your names are rather alike. Well, it's all turned out very well after all . . .'

As an apology it lacked a certain grace, but I took it that Verena had not had much practice in the art.

'Good meeting last night,' she said. 'Excellent turn-out. Not as many as last month, but we had a gardening expert then and that always pulls 'em in. I bought a plant from her afterwards—a pot plant. That's it over there . . .'

She gestured towards a large plant with flowers like yellow velvet.

'*Golden Dreams*, she called it,' said Verena. 'Do you like pot plants?'

She seemed to be looking at me very intently. I feared she was about to launch into a lecture on the care of pot plants.

'I prefer cut flowers,' I said hastily. 'You have to take such a lot of care of pot plants, and I haven't got green fingers. It's a good name, *Golden Dreams.*'

She laughed, and then said, 'Tell me, what do you do about your dreams, Miss Astolat? Do you put them into your books?'

'That's right,' I said lightly. 'Carefully disguised, of course . . .'

She shot me a suddenly shrewd look, and smiled.

'I thought your talk went down very well,' she said.

'Thank you,' I said. 'I certainly enjoyed the evening very much.'

'Glad to hear it,' said Verena. 'I'll write a piece for the local press about it. Mrs Robbins is supposed to handle our publicity, but she's not very inspired. "Miss Elaine Astolat gave a talk on *Romantic Novelists Today* which was warmly applauded. Mrs A proposed the vote of thanks and Mrs B seconded." End of publicity piece. I can do better than *that*!'

'Would it be too much trouble for you to send me a copy of the local paper with your piece in it?' I asked. 'I'd like to have it as a souvenir for my press cuttings collection.'

'Delighted,' said Verena gruffly.

We finished our breakfast, and I was about to rise from the table when Verena leaned across it, put her face very close to mine and said meaningfully, 'And what about a souvenir for *me*?'

She laid her hand on my arm, and I froze.

Was the woman making a pass at me?

We were alone in the house.

She was bigger than me, and very much stronger.

My mind raced.

I thought of the book I had brought with me, *Sweet Dreams of Arcady*.

'Would you like *Sweet Dreams* as a souvenir?' I asked.

'That's the ticket!' said Verena. 'Upstairs?'

'No!' I shouted.

She looked astonished, and I lowered my voice.

'I mean—oh, I mean it's in my bag—in the living-room . . .'

I turned and ran from the kitchen, flung open my bag, grabbed the book and ran back with it. To my surprise, Verena wasn't there.

I looked round for her cautiously, afraid she was going to jump on me.

Then I saw her through the window—she was out in the garden cutting roses with a pair of secateurs.

I withdrew to the living-room, fastened my bag and slipped on my coat, ready for immediate flight. I found the telephone and rang for a taxi to take me to the station right away. I didn't care how long I had to wait for a train at Bettesham. Anything would be better than being cooped up here with Verena, especially Verena armed with secateurs.

I could hear her moving about in the kitchen. She seemed to be taking her time.

Then I heard her coming towards me.

I swung round, tensed.

She stood smiling in the doorway of the living-room and held out a bunch of roses wrapped in tissue paper.

'Thought you might like these—remind you of us when you're in stuffy old London,' she said, and thrust the roses at me.

There was a ring at the door.

My taxi had arrived.

I was saved.

'They're gorgeous, Verena, thank you so much, sorry I have to dash,' I gabbled. 'And thank you for a wonderful evening and . . . and everything . . .'

I rushed out to the taxi and hurled myself into it.

As we drove away, Verena stood smiling in the porch, waving me farewell with her copy of *Sweet Dreams of Arcady*.

On my way to the station I called in at the newsagent's and ordered a copy of the local paper to be sent to me next week—just in case Verena forgot her promise.

When I reached home I took the roses out of their tissue paper. Verena had wrapped their stems in damp cotton wool to keep them fresh, and she'd wrapped a green and gold plastic bag from Marks and Spencer around the damp wool to keep the tissue paper dry. I was about to throw away the bag when I felt something inside it.

I opened the bag.

Inside was a note from Verena: '*Thanks for sweet dreams. Congratulations on excellent cover.*'

Plus enough ten-pound notes to pay for a shopping-trolleyload of *Sweet Dreams*.

I stood staring at them.

First things first, as Verena said. I put the roses into water. I put away my romantic finery. I slipped into a housecoat and made myself a pot of tea. And then I sat down and I *thought*.

Why should Verena have given me such a lot of money, and why had she mentioned the 'excellent cover'?

I got out a copy of *Sweet Dreams of Arcady* and looked closely at the cover. There didn't appear to be anything unusual about it. Just a standard picture of a man and a woman gazing into each other's eyes. Or—*was* it a man? It was just possible, by using a great deal of imagination, to mistake the man for a woman. But it required a great deal of imagination.

Could Verena be under the impression that I had presented her with a lesbian love-story?

And was that what Bunty had in mind when she talked about 'nasty things' being done by some of the Agency speakers? The thought of Bunty Beresford reminded me of the reception at the Royal Casterbridge—Verena calling 'Contessa!' and embracing a plump, baby-faced woman, who must have been the Contessa della Stola. I mustn't read too much into what was a perfectly normal, friendly gesture between two women. On the other hand . . . I recalled Verena's reaction when I said that I had 'deputized' for the Contessa, and how her manner had immediately become much more friendly. Was she hoping that I might deputize for the Contessa, not as a speaker, but in a rather different capacity?

If Bunty suspected Verena of having lesbian relationships with some of the speakers, then it was no wonder that she had been upset. To a woman of her age and upbringing it would have been a very shocking thing. And she would not express her fears in writing because, as she had said, 'You see, I'm not sure . . .' But she wanted to warn the Agency. I wondered if she had been able to do so before she died.

In any case, I supposed I ought to do so.

I would tell Philippa.

'*How* much did you say?' said Philippa.

I passed the green and gold shopping-bag across the desk to her and settled back to drink the coffee she'd had waiting for me on my arrival at Crispin Wharf House.

She opened the bag and spread the notes over her desk.

'H'mmmm,' she said, and looked at me pensively over the top of her spectacles. 'And I suppose you didn't . . .?'

'I did not!' I said indignantly.

'And what's the name of your book?'

'It's called *Sweet Dreams of Arcady*.'

'Heterosexual? Boy meets girl and so on?'

'Of course,' I said, and giggled. I had a sudden vision of my editor's face if I had offered her anything else.

There was a pause.

'Philippa,' I said, 'you remember Bunty Beresford—Verena's sister-in-law—she told me that she thought there was something nasty going on, and that she was going to warn Mary Michaelmas.'

'Bunty's dead!' said Philippa sharply. 'She died over a year ago at the Royal Casterbridge Hotel. I know. I was there.'

'So was I,' I said. 'Bunty was taken ill during the reception and I gave her a glass of water while she took a pill.'

'I didn't know that,' said Philippa. She looked thoughtful. 'What kind of pill did she take?'

'I—I don't know,' I said. 'I remember it was bright red —she made a little joke about "red for danger". She was much better after she'd taken it. She went back to the reception, and I saw her talking to Mary Michaelmas.'

'Mary didn't say anything to me about "something nasty" going on,' said Philippa. 'If she had, I'd have stopped it straight away, whatever it was.'

'So Bunty's warning didn't get through,' I said.

'No,' said Philippa. 'Mind you, we don't know for sure what it was that she wanted to warn Mary about. Let's face it, dear old Bunty was getting on, and it might have been something quite harmless that Mary wouldn't bother about. Anyhow, I'll talk to Mary about it as soon as she gets back from the studios. That should clear everything up.'

'Except . . .' I said, looking at the money spread over the desk.

Philippa thought for a few moments.

'Look,' she said, 'I tell you what I'll do. We shall all be going down to Bettesham soon—Julian and Mary are doing *A Lover and his Lass* as part of the Bettesham Festival—'

'Oh yes,' I said. 'I saw the poster on the station.'

'I'll be going with them,' said Philippa. 'I can run over to King's Martlet before the show to see Verena. If she doesn't come up with an acceptable explanation for the money I'll give it back to her—*and* I'll give her a piece of my mind to be getting on with. How would that do?'

'It's a bit embarrassing,' I mumbled, feeling myself going hot and cold all over at the thought of Philippa descending upon Verena like an angel with a flaming sword.

'If you feel badly about it, why don't you just send the money back to her and forget about it?' said Philippa.

'I think I'd rather do that,' I said.

I stuffed the notes back into the green and gold plastic bag, and then I stuffed the bag into one of the Agency's envelopes. On the way home I posted the money back to Verena.

But I didn't forget about it.

CHAPTER 10

RED FOR DANGER

I didn't forget about it. I just tucked it away in the back of my mind and got on with my new book. It was set in England in the time of James I, and a lot of the action took place around the Pool of London. If Darius had done nothing else for me, at least he had given me a setting for a story. Historical novels are not my line—I'd found that out with my dreadful story about the highwayman on Blackheath—but this one was going to be good—in fact, it was going to be my best ever. I roughed out the plot, and then I plunged into a mass of research for settings and costumes. Gradually the whole thing took shape, and at last I wrote the final page.

It was a warm afternoon, and before long I found myself half-dozing. All around me were the books I'd been using as reference material. I turned the pages drowsily, and for a long time sat staring at a picture of a dress embroidered with lover's knots. Idly I began to doodle knots in the margin of my notebook.

Knit, knot, knit, knot, the words sounded like the lazy ticking of a clock. Knit, knot, knit, knot . . . lots and lots and *lots* of knots . . . knit, knot, knit, knot. Rope knot . . . reef knot . . . Reef Knot Garden . . . Garden anagram danger . . . Red for danger . . . reefer danger . . . reefers! REEFERS!

I was out of my doze and fully awake now.

Cannabis!

That was the elusive memory that had tantalized me last week in the living-room at King's Martlet, a memory from my days as a student when the smart set used to smoke reefers, despite the fact that the smokers were always being found out because cannabis has such a distinctive smell.

Somewhere in that living-room there had been cannabis, its scent masked by the sweet fragrance of the pot-pourri. Smells from the kitchen of coffee and grilled bacon would have masked it even more.

I thought back to the house that had belonged at first to Bunty and her husband; then to the widowed Bunty sharing it with her sister-in-law; and now to Verena alone. I could read the signs easily enough. The old house and its furnishings spoke of prosperity before the war. Then Bunty's income dwindled—perhaps when her husband died—and she learned to make her things last. Even her clothes, I remembered, had been good but carefully preserved. Her bedroom, and the room where she entertained her friends, had been pleasant but old-fashioned. The bathroom, hardly ever seen by anyone outside the family, badly needed modernizing, but that had been beyond her means. Probably the kitchen had been in a similar state.

Then Bunty died, and everything passed to Verena. And in a very short time, Verena had spent a great deal of money on having her dream kitchen built.

According to the indiscreet Mrs Robbins, Bunty had not left very much money, so Verena could not have used her inheritance to pay for the kitchen. Where did the money come from? I had very little doubt that it came from peddling cannabis. A small amount, easily concealed, sold at a very high price to a few very high-class customers. Where, I wondered, did she get her supply? And even as I asked the question, I knew the answer. *She got it from some of the Supper Club speakers.*

That was what she meant when she asked me for a 'souvenir'. But why did she assume that I was carrying cannabis?

I thought back to the reception at the Royal Casterbridge Hotel over a year ago, when bookers wore rectangular badges and speakers wore round ones, and everybody knew at a glance which camp everybody belonged to, until I unwittingly wore the wrong badge and sabotaged the system. Was it possible that I had unknowingly 'worn the wrong badge' at King's Martlet by saying or doing something that led Verena to take me for one of her suppliers?

I thought back to the scene at breakfast. Verena had drawn my attention to a *pot* plant. She had told me that it was called *Golden Dreams*. She had spoken of her *dream* kitchen, and she had asked if I put my *dreams* into my books. I had agreed—'carefully disguised', I had added.

It looked as though 'dream' was some kind of password.

Then when Verena had asked me for a souvenir, I had offered her *Sweet Dreams of Arcady*! Well, that was what I meant. But I'd been scared of Verena, and what I actually said was, 'Would you like *Sweet Dreams* as a souvenir?'

You can't actually *hear* capital letters, so Verena would have heard, 'Would you like sweet dreams as a souvenir?' And because she was hoping for a discreetly coded reply to her discreetly coded question, she heard what she wanted to hear—an offer of sweet dreams—in other words, cannabis—'carefully disguised' in a book. She must have expected to find a neat little packet of cannabis under the dust-jacket. Hence the reference in her note to the 'excellent cover'—and hence the cash . . .

But Verena couldn't be the only person involved. Had anybody else ever expressed any interest in dreams? I took down my Talks file and read through my notes on each engagement.

November. Question: Can you remember your dreams?
Answer: No, they disappear too quickly.
January. Question: Do you dream in colour or monochrome?
Answer: In colour. What do you do?

There had been no follow-up to either of these. Perhaps I was imagining things. And yet . . . and yet . . . when I was having breakfast with Verena I had made a casual remark about the Dream Tower, and she had asked if I knew the Contessa della Stola. At the time it seemed like a complete change of subject, but was it? Could there be a connection between the 'dream' password and the Contessa?

Where had I heard about the Dream Tower? Of course! It was at Barrswood, on St Valentine's Day, *the day that I had deputized for the Contessa.* And it was after the meeting at Barrswood that my overnight bag had been stolen. And what was the only thing taken from it? A paperback book called *Dreams and Shadows.*

There had to be a connection. The Dream Tower—*Dreams and Shadows* at Barrswood, and then *Sweet Dreams of Arcady* at King's Martlet . . . And the connection must be the Contessa. She must be the cannabis carrier . . .

But why should the Rabbit assume that I was carrying cannabis at the Barrswood meeting just because my book had a title with the word 'dream' in it? Indeed, why had he turned up there at all? He wasn't the type of man to do anything without instructions from somebody higher up. So 'somebody higher up' had told him to attend the meeting. And that person had expected the Contessa to be the speaker. But I had deputized for the Contessa . . . and I had done so at the last moment. *So the person giving the orders didn't know that the Agency had changed the speaker.*

But—but the *Rabbit* must have known. He was at the meeting. He must have heard Mrs Winters announcing that the Contessa was indisposed and that I had taken her place . . . Then I remembered the bus-load of people who arrived after I had begun speaking—a bus-load which included the Rabbit. Most of the late-comers would have been told by their friends that I was deputizing for the Contessa. But the Rabbit had no friends. Nobody would have told him of the change. He thought I was the Contessa! When I did my reading, and when Mr Um asked me the name of the book, I had said '*Dreams and Shadows*' loud and clear. If I was right in my idea of the 'dream' password, and the system of coded questions and answers, then the Rabbit would have expected the book to contain a hidden supply of cannabis. When he heard me say, 'I've already promised it to a friend,' he must have thought that I was double-crossing him. So he followed me to the station, jumped on the train and grabbed the bag—and when the train stopped unexpectedly he just grabbed the book and jumped down on to the track.

He'd gone to a lot of trouble to steal a perfectly ordinary paperback. But that wasn't what he was hoping for. He was hoping for cannabis. He had to be in the same racket as Verena Gadsden.

Ought I to tell the police? I shrank from the very idea. I could imagine myself stumbling through my story to an incredulous sergeant, and I could imagine the look on his face when I admitted that I was a romantic novelist . . .

I'd better ring Philippa. She at least would not dismiss me out of hand. But before I could ring her, the postman delivered a bright yellow padded envelope postmarked 'Barrswood'. Inside was a letter from Mrs Winters, the Secretary of the Barrswood Literary Society.

Dear Miss Astolat,

I enclose a review of your talk and the photograph which appeared in our local paper. I also enclose a set of photographs taken at our St Valentine's Day party. I must apologize for the delay, but most of our photographers had to wait until they had used up their complete rolls of film before sending the pictures to be developed and printed. I have identified most of the people, and you will find their names on the back of the pictures.

Mrs Potter asks me to say that she took the rather odd 'knife' picture because she thought it made an interesting composition.

Thank you very much for a delightful evening.

Yours sincerely,
Enid Winters.

I read the review, which informed everybody that Miss Elaine Astolat gave a very interesting talk about *Romantic Novelists Today* and afterwards cut the cake at the St Valentine's Day party (see picture on page 4), and turned to the photographs.

They were in a wallet of clear plastic envelopes, each one containing a colour photograph. There were several excellent close-ups of the cake with the red satin heart, several pictures of me pretending to cut the cake while the guests raised their glasses self-consciously; several pictures of the Secretary's husband down on one knee offering me the red satin heart; and then a lot of general shots of the party after I had left. And at the end, a collection of black and white pictures taken by the elderly lady with the Leica.

The very last one was the 'interesting composition' mentioned by Mrs Winters.

It must have been taken when the old lady was sitting down and when I was practising with the cake-knife before the ceremony began, because in the foreground was my hand holding the knife like the Sword of Damocles, and, in the background, two men deep in conversation, blithely unaware of the threat apparently hanging over them. But what interested me most about the picture was not the composition, arresting though it was. The interesting thing was the two men in the background. They were the Rabbit and the man in the raincoat—Mr Um.

And now for the first time I realized that the rabbit had not been the only person involved in stealing my bag. I was prepared to swear that Mr Um had been the Rabbit's accomplice, if not the prime mover. I remembered a good many things. Mr Um at Question Time asking if he could buy *Dreams and Shadows*. Then Mr Um standing beside me at the party and whispering 'I don't mind paying a bit extra for it . . .' Mr Um at Barrswood station, helping me on to the train, where his job had been to place my bag where the Rabbit could get at it easily, and to hold my attention with his nasty little bodice-ripper while the bag was being stolen. And when I chased the Rabbit and was gaining on him, Mr Um lurched into me, accidentally on purpose, and knocked me off my balance. And like the Rabbit, Mr Um had arrived by the late bus, and hadn't heard the announcement of the change of speaker. Like the Rabbit, he mistook me for the Contessa. I remembered now, he'd even called me 'Contessa' on the train. When I pulled the communication cord he said something like, 'Now you've done it, Contessa!' and when I replied 'I'm not the Contessa' he had run off, saying he was going to get the guard.

And then—what?

I thought of the Rabbit leaping down the steps of the footbridge at Barrswood station—*he'd* have had no trouble in jumping down on to the track from the stationary train after the robbery. But Mr Um? He wasn't built for gymnastics. I wondered what he had done. Had he jumped down from the train at the same time as the Rabbit, or had he simply hidden in a toilet and descended in a more orthodox manner at the first station?

And I remembered another thing. At the party, when Mr Um noticed the photographers gathering, he had disappeared. Why had he done that? He had said he didn't want to spoil the picture, and had backed modestly away. But Mr Um was under the impression that I was the Contessa, a carrier of cannabis. What a nightmare for any self-respecting drugs dealer, to be caught talking to a person he took to be a drugs carrier, and to be caught doing so by the massed cameras of the Barrswood Literary Society!

Wait a minute though! Mr Um *had* been caught—by the man with the Polaroid camera. *He* had taken his picture before the other photographers were ready, and his picture showed Mr Um talking to me as I stood by the cake. I had been given the photograph as I left the party. I'd waved it in the air to show everybody. I'd slipped it into my overnight bag—and I'd never seen it again. I could guess where it had gone—into the night with *Dreams and Shadows*.

I reached for the phone.

'Mrs Winters? This is Elaine Astolat. Thank you so much for sending me the pictures of the St Valentine's Day party—'

'It's good of you to ring, Miss Astolat. I'm sorry it's taken so long to get the set together, but it was a lovely evening and everyone's very pleased to have the pictures as souvenirs—'

'Mrs Winters—that black-and-white picture—the one with the interesting composition of the knife hanging over the heads of the two men—'

'Oh dear, Miss Astolat, I'm afraid it *does* look a bit gruesome, I hope you didn't mind—'

'I think it's perfectly splendid,' I said. 'But can you tell me anything about the two men? Was it their first visit to the Society?'

Mrs Winters thought briefly.

'I'm sorry, Miss Astolat, I really don't know. I know that neither of them is a member of the Society, but I have a feeling that I'd seen them at earlier meetings. I do know that they haven't attended any meetings since then. Is it very important?'

'I think it may be,' I said. 'Is there any way of finding out?'

'Well,' said Mrs Winters, 'Mrs Potter might know. She's our Treasurer—she sits at the door and takes people's money as they arrive. She might remember them. Would you like me to ask her?'

'They came with several other people on a bus that was late,' I said. 'So she might remember that. Could you perhaps give me her phone number so that I can call her direct?'

'Oh, no need for that,' said Mrs Winters. 'Mrs Potter will be here before long—I'll call you back as soon as she gets here. 'Bye now . . .'

Within half an hour Mrs Potter came on the line. I had a mental picture of an old grey heron standing hunched on one leg, clutching the phone in a crooked claw.

'I remember the two men, Miss Astolat—they came in with the rest of the people on the bus that was late. I don't know their names, but they'd certainly been to some of the earlier meetings this season. One of them always wore a raincoat.'

'Do you remember which meetings?' I asked.

'They were here for—wait a minute—September and December.'

'And had you ever seen them together before?'

'No,' she said. 'I'd always assumed they were complete strangers to each other, as they were to the rest of us. And then when I went to take a picture of you practising with

the knife—I hope you didn't mind that, but I thought it
looked interesting—then suddenly I noticed these two men
in the background talking together as though they knew
each other quite well.'

'Did you notice what happened after that?' I asked. 'Was
that the only time you saw them together?'

'Yes,' she said. 'And they were only speaking for a few
minutes—afterwards they ignored each other completely.'

'Do you remember who the speaker was at the September
meeting?' I asked.

'September . . .' said Mrs Potter. 'Yes. September was
Indoor Gardening. The speaker—I've forgotten her name
but Mrs Winters would know—she brought a lot of pot
plants and sink gardens to show us. She sold quite a lot of
them but—oh yes, I've just remembered—she said the sink
gardens were rather heavy, and the man in the raincoat
helped her to carry the unsold ones back to her car. I was
a bit surprised, because he didn't look the helpful kind, but
it just shows how wrong you can be.'

'The December meeting,' I said. 'Was that the one with
the candle-maker?'

'Yes,' she said. 'He sold a lot of them, especially the
Christmassy ones.'

'Was he the one with the Dream Tower candle? I said.

'That's right,' said Mrs Potter. 'It was a splendid affair,
all purple and orange swirls. The man in the raincoat helped
him to carry it out to his car afterwards. He looked so funny,
carrying the Dream Tower as if it was a baby . . .'

'Do you know if he bought it?' I asked.

'No, I don't know that,' said Mrs Potter. 'I'm sorry I
can't be more helpful.'

'Mrs Potter,' I said, 'you've been very helpful indeed.
Thank you for giving me so much of your time. Goodbye.'

I slipped the wallet of photographs into the Barrswood
folder in the Talks file. As I did so, my hand touched
something soft—it was the red satin heart. I pulled it out

and stood looking down at it, feeling sure that it was trying
to tell me something.

Heart.

Red.

Red for danger . . .

And then I made the connection.

Bunty Beresford had a bad *heart*.

Bunty Beresford took a *red* pill.

Bunty Beresford died.

Was it possible that she died, not because of heart trouble
as I'd thought, but because of that red pill?

Was it a case of—*murder?*

My mind began to race. Bunty intended to warn Mary
Michaelmas that 'something nasty' was going on. And was
that 'something nasty' the distribution of cannabis? Could
she have been murdered to keep her mouth shut?

The thought had not occurred to me before. Why should
it? Nobody would commit murder to keep lesbian affairs a
secret. But to keep *drug-trafficking* secret . . .? That might
well be a reason for murder . . .

I slowed down, and tried to visualize the scene at the
Royal Casterbridge Hotel. Bunty gasping for breath, open-
ing her pill-box, taking out the red pill and swallowing it.
Verena coming in and saying, 'Have you taken your pill?'
So she knew there was only one pill in the box for Bunty to take.

And soon afterwards, Bunty died . . .

Who was the person most likely to know where Bunty
kept her pills?

Verena Gadsden, who lived in the same house.

Who was the person with the best opportunity of poison-
ing the pill?

Verena Gadsden.

And who was the person with the best reason for wanting
to stop Bunty's mouth?

Verena Gadsden.

*

It occurred to me that it was just as well that I was out of Verena's reach. The woman was angry, and frightened, and she was dangerous. If she could kill Bunty—and I had no doubt of that now—then she would have no compunction about killing me.

As long as I was in London and she was in King's Martlet, I was safe. I would take very good care not to go anywhere near King's Martlet. But—supposing Verena came to London and found out where I lived? I felt a little stab of fear.

Then I remembered the envelope in which I had returned the money to her. It carried the Crispin Speakers' Agency emblem of a silver swan. So Verena would guess that I had told Philippa about the money. And by doing that, I had unwittingly put Philippa's life in danger as well as my own.

With a sense of shock I recalled Philippa saying something about visiting Verena when Julian and Mary performed *A Lover and his Lass* at Bettesham.

When would she be going? I could remember seeing the poster at Bettesham station, but I'd taken no note of the date of the performance.

I felt suddenly sick and very, very cold.

Whatever happened, I must stop Philippa going to King's Martlet . . .

CHAPTER 11

RED SKY AT NIGHT

My hand was shaking as I dialled Philippa's number.

I waited, and waited, and waited.

'Come on, Philippa,' I muttered. 'Come on, Philippa, where are you?'

Then, 'Crispin Speakers' Agency,' said a voice at last. A man's voice.

'Where's Philippa?' I shouted.

'Philippa's not here at the moment. Can I help you? This is Darius Underwood speaking.'

Darius!

So he'd come back from Marrakech . . .

The world seemed suddenly a little brighter.

'Darius, this is Elaine Astolat. I don't know if you remember me . . .?'

'Of course I remember you,' he said. 'Reef Knot Garden. You're the little girl who writes romantic novels about highwaymen on Blackheath . . .'

I seethed. What a terrible memory the man had.

'. . . and you don't smile very often, but when you do, your whole face lights up. Of course I remember you.'

I stopped seething. He had quite a good memory after all.

'Now, what's the problem?' he said.

'Darius, I'm terribly worried about Philippa. Do you know where she is?'

'Probably in the bar of the Six Bells in Danesborough knocking back a gin and tonic,' said Darius.

'Danesborough?' I said, surprised. 'But that's in Yorkshire.'

'Julian and Mary are doing *A Lover and his Lass* as part of the Danesborough Festival,' he said. 'Philippa's there with them.'

'When did you see her last?'

'This morning,' he said. He sounded a little impatient with all my questions.

So Philippa was safe! I nearly wept with relief.

'Astolat!' said Darius sharply. 'Are you still there? Are you all right?'

'Darius,' I said, 'I've got to talk to Philippa as soon as she gets back from Danesborough. I've got to warn her—it's a matter of life or death.'

'Come over here and tell me about it,' said Darius. 'I'm working on the *Silver Swan*—that's why I was a bit slow answering the phone. I'll leave the little side gate open for you.'

'I'm on my way,' I said.

All the same, I stopped long enough to change into a new, pretty summer dress (not from Bambinetta!), all broderie anglaise and frilly lace. I wasn't going to let Darius see me in my old working clothes. If Philippa was safe in Yorkshire there was no great rush.

I took the short cut through Magpie Lane, and as I passed the Reef Knot Garden I saw that the three reef knots were still standing high up on the top tier, while the pile of cables near the entrance still looked like a skein of wool with a knitting needle stuck into it. Even the red oil drum was still propping up the knitting needle. Nothing seemed to have changed. The sunset lit up the high overhead walkways and lent a warm glow to the old grey warehouses. They were all closed and silent now, and the sunset reflected in their windows made them look as though they were on fire. And there, at the end of Magpie Lane, was Crispin Wharf House. Its familiar shape and its warm, spicy smell made me feel that I was coming home. I ducked down the little side alley, brushing against the honeysuckle on the wall, and hurried through the open gate and out on to the little landing-stage.

The sunset had coloured even the cold grey waters of the Thames, and high above me small fluffy clouds were tinged with pink, while beyond Tower Bridge the whole sky was ablaze. 'Red sky at night, Shepherd's delight.' Tomorrow would be a lovely day. And today wasn't so bad . . .

Darius was working on the deck of the *Silver Swan*, but as soon as he saw me he jumped on to the little landing-stage and came towards me, wiping his hands on a rag which he tossed back on to the boat. He was in working gear—an old blue sports shirt open at the throat, and a pair of oil-stained shorts. He looked just as I remembered him.

My heart was pounding, and something seemed to have happened to my breathing.

And he—for the first time he was seeing the new Astolat in a new, pretty dress. He put out his hand towards me, and for a long time we stood there on the little white landing-stage just looking at each other.

'Astolat! My dear girl, you're shaking like a leaf! Here, sit down and tell me what the matter is . . .'

I let him guide me towards one of the white canvas chairs. His bare arm brushed against my hand, and we sprang apart almost guiltily. He stood looking down at me for a few moments, then he swung a bucket off the deck of the *Silver Swan*, up-ended it and sat down on it.

'That doesn't look very comfortable,' I said, trying to sound my normal self.

'It'll do,' he said. 'Old Philippa would give me hell if I got oil-stains on one of Julian's deckchairs.'

I laughed a little shakily.

'That's better,' he said. 'Now, take a deep breath, begin at the beginning, and tell me what's bothering you.'

With an effort I dragged my mind back to drug-trafficking and other minor matters.

'First of all,' I said as calmly as I could, 'I think the Agency is being used as a front for a drugs racket.'

Darius raised his eyebrows, but he didn't interrupt.

'The Agency supplies speakers to societies and clubs all over the country. Some of the speakers are doing more than just giving talks—they are also acting as couriers for a drugs ring. You know how it is—after you've given your talk, people come up to you and ask if you have any copies of your books for sale—and if you have, may they buy one and will you autograph it?'

Darius nodded.

'Some speakers sell their books—or whatever it is they're

talking about. The woman who talks about pot plants, the man who demonstrates the art of making candles—any of them may sell some of their things after their talk.'

I paused, but Darius didn't say anything.

'It would be very easy,' I said, 'to hide a small plastic envelope of cannabis powder at the base of a pot plant, or inside the dust-jacket of a book, or inside a lump of coloured wax.'

Darius stared at me.

'Well, of course, it *could* be done,' he said at last. 'But— literary societies and luncheon clubs as a front for a drugs ring! Oh, come off it, Astolat! Their members are the most respectable, law-abiding people you could hope to meet—'

'That's exactly why they make such good cover,' I said. 'They're all nice people—and it's because they're so nice that it would be easy to take advantage of them. It's not that the societies are being *run* as a cover for drug-peddling, but that some of them have been—well—infiltrated.'

'How d'you mean?' said Darius.

'I don't know exactly how it's done,' I said, 'but I'm quite sure it *is* done. Drugs and money often change hands after a meeting.'

'But the money that changes hands even for a minute quantity of a drug would be very high,' said Darius. 'I mean, it's one thing to pay a small amount for a book or a plant or a lump of wax—it's a very different thing to pay for a supply of cannabis. The genuine members would be sure to notice if anybody handed over fistfuls of notes to a speaker.'

'Payment doesn't have to happen in full view of every-body,' I said. 'The speaker could ask the buyer to lend a hand carrying things to the car, and the handover could take place in the car park. Something like that.'

'But Astolat, I've met quite a lot of these speakers, and I'll swear they're perfectly genuine. They may be slightly nutty—they all seem to think their particular subject is the hub of the universe—but I cannot believe that any of them would be involved in anything remotely illegal—and certainly not drug trafficking! Whatever gave you such an idea?'

'In February,' I said, 'I gave a talk to a Literary Society. It was St Valentine's Day, and after the talk they had a party, and they asked me to cut their special St Valentine's Day cake.'

'Don't tell me there was cannabis in the cake,' said Darius.

I glared at him. This was a serious matter.

'During my talk,' I said, 'I read some passages from one of my books called *Dreams and Shadows* and a man asked if he could buy it—I hate selling books, so I told him that my copy was promised to somebody else but that he could get one at any bookshop. And I put the book into my overnight bag. Then when I went to the station to catch the train back to London, the man was waiting for me on the platform, helped me on to the train, carried my overnight bag and stowed it behind my seat where I couldn't keep my eye on it. He tried to hold my attention by showing me a dreadful manuscript he said he'd written, and while I was looking at that, I saw another man pick up my bag and run off with it.'

'What did you do?' asked Darius.

'I ran after him,' I said. 'The man with the manuscript pretended to be helping me, but in fact he hindered me, so I pulled the communication cord and the train stopped.'

Darius laughed.

'You don't do things by halves, do you?' he said.

I looked at him coldly.

'The man with the bag disappeared,' I said, 'and so did the man with the manuscript, though I didn't find that out until much later. The guard came along, and eventually he found my bag and returned it to me . . .'

'Anything missing?' asked Darius.

'The paperback book,' I said. 'But the notebooks for my new story were safe.'

'Did you make an official complaint?' said Darius.

'No. Once I'd got my notebooks back I didn't care about anything else. Besides, I didn't want to hold the train up, it was late and I just wanted to get back home.'

'But, Astolat, what has all this got to do with cannabis?'

'The name of my book was *Dreams and Shadows*,' I said. 'And I think the people in the racket are using the word "dream" as some kind of password.'

I could see that Darius was not impressed.

'Do you know the names of the two men?' he asked.

'No,' I said. 'I just called them the Rabbit and Mr Um. They were strangers to everybody in the Literary Society . . .'

'Could you identify them?' he asked.

'Yes,' I said. 'There were lots of people taking photographs of the cake-cutting business. One man took a Polaroid picture of me with Mr Um standing beside me— I put the photograph into my overnight bag.'

'Have you still got it?' asked Darius.

'No,' I said. 'It disappeared with the paperback.'

Darius raised his eyes to heaven.

'So you see,' I said, 'they knew that it was evidence.'

'Oh really, Astolat!' said Darius.

'Ah, but wait,' I said. 'The Secretary of the Society has just sent me a whole collection of pictures of the party— they only arrived today. And one picture shows the two men talking together—Mr Um and the Rabbit.'

'Have you got it with you?' he asked.

'I've got them all,' I said.

I took the wallet out of my handbag, and gave it to him. He looked through the pictures, and I sat quietly and looked at him. Behind him, the *Silver Swan* bobbed at her moorings, red sunlight flashing from the cabin windows.

'You look very professional cutting that cake,' he said.

'Actually the cake had already been cut,' I said. 'I just had to pretend.'

'And who's the chap on his knees offering you his heart?'

'He's the husband of the Society's Secretary,' I said. 'They were so long taking those pictures I thought I was going to miss my train.'

'And the two villains—where are they?'

'They're in the black-and-white pictures at the back,' I said.

He looked through the black-and-white pictures.

'These are very good,' he said. 'But where—oh!'

He had seen the picture of the two men under the Sword of Damocles.

'I take it these are your two villains?'

'Yes,' I said.

'They're not very handsome, and they certainly look as though they were a bit out of place,' said Darius.

'The man in the raincoat is Mr Um—the one who showed me the manuscript,' I said eagerly. 'And that one's the Rabbit, the one who actually stole the bag.'

Darius laid the wallet of pictures down on a chair, and then he looked at me rather sternly.

'Astolat, all that these pictures prove is that you attended a St Valentine's Day party, and that among those present were two strangers known to you as Mr Um and the Rabbit. They might be a pair of villains—they might equally well be a couple of blameless citizens.'

'Darius!' I cried.

He looked very thoughtful.

'Astolat,' he said at last, 'how do you write your novels? Which comes first, character or plot?'

I wondered why he'd changed the subject.

'First I get my characters,' I said, 'and then they tell me the story.'

'And where do you find your characters?'

'I—I don't really know,' I said. 'Sometimes it's just somebody I see in the street, or on the bus or the train—or on television. It might even be a photograph in a magazine

or a newspaper—or a photograph album. I put them down
in my notebook, or I file them away in my subconscious—
and when they're ready, they'll start to tell me their story.
At least, I suppose it's my own imagination that produces
the story, but it feels as though the characters are doing
it . . .'

'Are you sure that your imagination isn't producing a
story about Mr Um and the Rabbit?' he asked. 'This is
a very dramatic picture—two men under the Sword of
Damocles—are you sure this didn't give you the idea about
drug-traffickers and train thieves? *Are you sure you're not making
the whole thing up?*'

CHAPTER 12

THE SPIDER

'I am not making it up!' I said furiously. 'I only got that
picture today—but I've got all my notes about the Rabbit
and Mr Um in the report that I wrote about the meeting
—and I wrote *that* down in the train on my way home on
February 14th!'

'Have you got your notes with you?' he asked.

'No, I have not,' I said. 'But they wouldn't be of any use
to you because they're all written in shorthand. But *I* know
they're there, and *I* can read them. Do you want me to send
you a transcript?'

'All right, calm down,' said Darius. 'I only said—'

'I didn't connect Mr Um with the Rabbit until I saw
that picture—and I didn't connect either of them with
drug-trafficking until this afternoon.'

'And what happened this afternoon?' asked Darius.

'I suddenly realized that the Agency was being used as a
cover—'

'What brought you to that realization? Not the subconscious again?'

Darius was not what I would call a sympathetic audience. 'Look,' I said, 'last week I gave a talk at a club in the country, and I made an overnight stay at the President's house—their President always offers hospitality to the speaker, it's one of their unwritten rules. And the next morning—Wednesday—the President gave me a lot of money under—well, under rather odd circumstances. I'm sure the money was meant to be in payment for cannabis. There was certainly a smell of the stuff about the house. You can't mistake it once you've smelt it.'

'And when have you used cannabis?' asked Darius softly.

'I've never used it,' I said. 'But I can recognize it. When I was a student quite a lot of people smoked pot. It was rather the "in" thing to do.'

'But you didn't do it?'

'No,' I said. 'I was never one of the "in" groups.'

I felt myself blushing uncomfortably at the memory. I'd always longed to be a member of one of the 'in' groups, but they'd never taken any notice of me.

'If they had asked you to smoke pot, would you have done it?'

I thought for a while.

'Almost certainly yes,' I said at last. 'When you're young and terribly unsure of yourself, you're very vulnerable. Yes, I think I should have done. I wanted so much to conform to what the leaders were doing.'

'And now?' he said.

'Oh no,' I said.

'Suppose somebody you loved asked you to try cannabis?' he said.

'No,' I said.

'Somebody you loved very much, who was hooked on the stuff, and begged you to help him—perhaps begged you to try it to understand how he felt?'

He looked at me very earnestly.

'No,' I said. 'That would only mean two of us getting hooked.'

Darius seemed to relax a little.

'Stick to that, Astolat,' he said. 'But listen, my dear, seriously, if ever you smell cannabis again, put on your running shoes and get away fast. Drug-traffickers are not nice people to be mixed up with, and you might get hurt. Promise me?'

He laid his hand on mine and our eyes met. Once more I could feel my heart thumping.

'I promise,' I said.

'And now,' he said, smiling, 'who do you think is the spider at the heart of this web?'

I had a sudden vision of the beautiful, glittering spider's web at the Christmas Fair, with the shrouded body of the dead fly, and once again I felt a little shiver run through me. Then I pulled myself together and made myself talk calmly.

'You mean—who's running the whole show?' I said. 'I've no idea. I haven't even tried to work that one out.'

'Well, who was the villain who gave you the money last Wednesday?'

'Her name,' I said carefully, 'is Verena Gadsden.'

Darius threw back his head and roared with laughter. I was annoyed, but all the same I couldn't help noticing how delightfully his eyes crinkled at the corners.

'Verena Gadsden?' he said at last. 'The old trout down at King's Martlet?'

'You know her?' I said, astonished.

'Well, I met her for a few minutes last Saturday—Julian and Mary were doing *A Lover and his Lass* for the Bettesham Festival—'

'Last Saturday!' I said.

'—and old Philippa was masterminding everything for them as usual. I drove them all down to Bettesham, and when we got there they wanted to call on Verena, so I took them on to King's Martlet. That's when I met Verena. She certainly didn't look like a master criminal to me!'

A great weight was lifted from my shoulders. Philippa had visited Verena and had come away again unscathed.

'Did Philippa say anything about Verena giving me all that money?'

'She certainly didn't mention it going down in the car.'

'Oh, I'm so glad,' I said. 'I was afraid Verena might do Philippa some harm.'

Darius looked at me.

'Verena's a dangerous woman,' I went on. 'I'm sure she's involved in the drugs racket—and I *think* she murdered her sister-in-law.'

Darius looked thoroughly impatient.

'Oh, really, Astolat, *I* think this is your imagination at work again. What evidence have you got for all this drug-smuggling?'

'I *did* smell cannabis,' I said stubbornly. 'I *did* see the Dream Tower candle in Verena's kitchen, she *did* ask me for a souvenir, and she *did* give me all that money. It was wrapped around a bunch of roses from her garden.'

'And where is it now?' he said.

'I posted it back to her,' I said.

'Oh, Astolat!' said Darius, exasperated.

'I showed it to Philippa,' I said, 'and she offered to take it back to Verena and tick her off about it, but I felt a bit embarrassed and I said I'd send the money back myself— and I did.'

It sounded rather a thin story, even to me.

'So you've no evidence at all,' said Darius.

'N-no,' I said.

'And what's all this about murdering her sister-in-law?'

'Verena's sister-in-law was Bunty Beresford,' I said. 'You remember—the old lady who died at the Royal Casterbridge reception last year.'

His face became serious.

'Of course I remember her,' he said. 'I carried her out. But what makes you think she was murdered?'

'I met Bunty earlier that morning,' I said. 'She told me she was going to warn Mary Michaelmas that "something nasty" was going on in the Agency. But before she could warn Mary, Bunty died.'

'It seemed a perfectly natural death,' said Darius.

'Bunty was feeling ill early on at the reception,' I said. 'I gave her a glass of water, and she took a pill—a bright red pill—and she had a little rest, and then Verena came in and said 'Have you taken your pill?' She hustled Bunty back to the reception. And not long afterwards, Bunty died. I'm sure the pill was poisoned, and I'm sure Verena did it.'

'If the old lady was worried and unwell, the whole thing might have been too much for her heart,' said Darius. 'Really, Astolat, I think your imagination has been working overtime.'

'It was murder,' I said. 'I *know* it was. And—oh, Darius! I've just realized . . . I gave Bunty a glass of water and helped her to take that red pill! Don't you see—*I helped Verena to kill Bunty!*'

In my mind's eye I could see dear, shaky little Bunty taking out the pill, taking a sip of water from the glass I offered her, and swallowing the pill. My throat felt very tight, and I could feel tears starting to well up. I tried to blink them back, but it was no use.

'Oh, D-Darius,' I said, 'I'm afraid I'm going to cry . . .'

And I burst into tears.

'Ohhhhh dear,' I said helplessly, 'I h-haven't g-got a handkerchief. C-could you . . .?'

'Here,' said Darius. He sounded alarmed. 'Have this.'

He pulled me to my feet and thrust a handkerchief into my hand.

'Th-thank you,' I sobbed.

I mopped my eyes and blew my nose.

Rose-pink clouds went cartwheeling across the sky, the landing-stage dropped from under me like a descending lift, and the *Silver Swan* spun like a top. On the far bank of the river, wharves and warehouses lurched sideways . . .

'Hey! said Darius.

His arms went round me, and I could feel his heart thumping against my cheek.

I held on to him until the landing-stage was once more firm beneath my feet—or only a very little longer.

Slowly the sky and the Thames and the *Silver Swan* returned to normal.

'I-I'm s-sorry,' I gasped. 'I've—I've g-got to go home . . .'

Away to the west, Tower Bridge stood stark as a guillotine against the blood-red sunset.

I don't know how I got home that evening. Perhaps I took a taxi, perhaps I caught a bus, perhaps I just ran all the way. I remember staggering up the stairs on legs that seemed to be made of cotton-wool, unlocking the door with hands that trembled and shook, and almost falling into the flat. I slammed the door behind me, put up the chain and shot the bolt. But I didn't let go of the handkerchief that Darius had given me.

A handkerchief that smelt, unmistakably, of cannabis.

And now at last I understood the significance of a lot of things. There was a drugs racket all right, and it was run from Crispin Wharf House itself! The scent of spices surrounding the old warehouse was an essential part of the scheme, masking the smell of cannabis just as effectively as Bunty's pot-pourri had done at King's Martlet. And in addition to the spices, there was always the smell of freshly roasted coffee about the place to confuse things. Only a trained sniffer dog would have been able to trace the cannabis, and there weren't many of them around Crispin Wharf Street.

Like the craftsmen of Magpie Lane, the Crispin Speakers' Agency was running a cottage industry. Not a big racket, not a Mafia kind of set-up. Just a few people, dealing in quite small quantities, and making a nice little tax-free addition to their incomes, enough to enable them to build their dream kitchen, as Verena had done, or to run a boat like the *Silver Swan*. But at the end of the line were the flies caught in the spider's web, the poor silly devils hooked on the stuff, ruining themselves and their families to keep the nice little cottage industry ticking over.

But if the Agency was the headquarters of the racket, then Julian and Mary and Philippa must be involved, mustn't they? I thought long and hard about that.

It was just possible that Julian and Mary didn't know anything about it. Mary was too tied up with her TV chat show to pay much attention to the affairs of the Agency, even if she understood them, and as far as I could make out, Julian wouldn't notice anything that wasn't reflected in his mirror.

But Philippa—*she* was the brains of the outfit. She had the run of Crispin Wharf House. She would know which of the speakers might be prepared to distribute drugs in return for some no-questions-asked money. She would know who the buyers were. She organized the speakers' engagements. People like me provided a nice, innocent front for the inner ring of drug-pushers, and the clubs and societies provided a nice, innocent setting for the exchange of drugs and money. And the organizer, the one who pulled the strings, was Philippa.

No wonder there'd been an upset on St Valentine's Day when the Contessa was indisposed! Julian had arranged for me to take her place, unaware that Philippa had already made arrangements for the Rabbit and Mr Um to collect a supply of cannabis from her. Philippa was away that day, so she hadn't been able to stop the Rabbit and Mr Um turning up at the meeting. I wondered what had happened when Philippa found out . . .

But what could I do about it? As Darius had said, what evidence had I got? Even if I still had Verena's wads of ten-pound notes in the green and gold plastic bag, it would hardly prove that I was telling the truth. The whole point of ten-pound notes is that they cannot be traced—I might have drawn the whole lot from my bank myself. And the green and gold plastic bag from Marks and Spencer was hardly a one-off.

But of course I hadn't got the money. Thanks to Philippa, I had destroyed even that flimsy piece of evidence. And I had been afraid that Verena would harm Philippa! What a fool I was. Of course they were in it together.

There was one piece of evidence in my hands—the handkerchief with the smell of cannabis. There was no way I could prove that it came from Crispin Wharf House. But there was no way I could get away from the fact that it *did* come from there, and that Darius had given it to me.

Was *he* in it too? Oh, please God, not Darius . . .

But a small voice nagged away at me—*somebody* must bring the drugs into the country. Who? Who but the man who had come to the Royal Casterbridge Hotel straight from the airport and had handed a well-travelled overnight bag to Philippa Preston. The man who was for ever on his travels to Marrakech, to Anatolia, to Karachi—even *I* could remember seeing the names of those places in newspaper reports about drug-trafficking.

The handkerchief might belong to one of the others.

It didn't *have* to belong to Darius.

But in the end I had to face facts.

It didn't matter a damn *who* owned the handkerchief. The person who brought the cannabis into England had to be Darius.

And I was in love with him.

CHAPTER 13

THE BENDING SICKLE

Next morning, the post arrived, and with it a copy of the King's Martlet *Sentinel*, sent to me by the local newsagent. Verena had doubtless overlooked her promise to send me the paper, and in the circumstances I could hardly blame her. I wondered if she had also overlooked her promise to send the paper a review of my talk. Well, this would take my mind off Darius for a few minutes . . .

In spite of myself, I turned the pages eagerly, cursing as the ink blackened my fingers. Somewhere on the inside pages there should be *something* . . . The people of King's Martlet were holding garden parties and fun days and car boot sales and—ah yes, there it was—Ladies' Supper Club.

There was a full house at the Ladies' Supper Club when Miss Elaine Astolat gave a talk on *Rheumatic Novelists Today*. After touching on various aspects of her subject, she concluded with a reading from her latest book, *Wet Dreams of Arcady*, which was warmly applauded.

I flung the paper away with a yell of rage. *Rheumatic Novelists . . . Wet Dreams . . .*! Was this Verena's revenge, or just the local printers having fun? I stamped about and cursed everybody I could think of. Then I cooled down a little, decided that it would at least make an addition to my Black Museum of press cuttings, grabbed a pair of scissors and took up the paper again. I cut out the offending review, folded the paper tidily and dropped it on top of others standing ready for the wastepaper collection.

For the first time I noticed the front page with its headlines:

LOCAL RESIDENTS' DEARTH
Shack for Cleaner

Had a dearth of houses for the local residents condemned a cleaner to live in a shack? What kind of front page story was that? There was a blurred photograph of a house. It didn't look much like a shack. Suddenly I recognized it as Bunty's house. Or rather, Verena's. I began to read the story.

> Local cleaner Mrs Marlene Boardman (60), of Martlets Ambo, had a nasty shock when she went to the house of her employer, Mrs Verena Gadsden, on Wednesday morning. Receiving no reply to her repeated knocking at the front door, she went round to the back of the house and found the body of Mrs Gadsden lying in the garden. Police were called, and preliminary investigations lead them to believe that Mrs Gadsden had been dead for several days.

I could feel the hairs at the nape of my neck rising, and I sat down, shocked and sickened. My mind refused to function. All I could see was Verena smiling and waving goodbye from the porch, the green and gold bag of banknotes wrapped round the roses, and Tower Bridge standing like a guillotine, black against the red sky. It was a fine summer morning, but I was shivering with cold.

Darius had taken Julian, Mary and Philippa to visit Verena last Saturday.

Had she been alive when they left?

I looked at the paper's date of publication. Thursday. And Verena had been found the previous day, Wednesday. Today was Saturday. Somebody at King's Martlet must

know more about Verena's death by now. Police ... but
they would hardly give information to a stranger. *Nobody*
would give information to a stranger. Was there anybody
in King's Martlet who would not regard me as a stranger?
Of course! The secretary of the Ladies' Supper Club, the
delightfully indiscreet Mrs Robbins. I rushed to my engagements file and looked up our correspondence. Mrs Robbins's
telephone number was at the top of the booking form. I rang
several times, but her number seemed to be permanently
engaged. Then suddenly I got through.

'Mrs Robbins? This is Elaine Astolat and—'

There was no need to explain why I was calling. Mrs
Robbins plunged into her story at once, so fluently that
I felt sure she had told it many times. No doubt that
was why her telephone had been engaged for such a long
time.

'Verena Gadsden—yes, a terrible shock for us all. Poor
Mrs Boardman—that's Verena's cleaning lady—she found
her—she came over here to my house to telephone the
police. She was in a terrible state—well, you can imagine
it, can't you? I was in the middle of baking cakes for the
Summer Fair, but of course I just dropped everything and
we had a cup of tea together.'

'Have they any idea when it happened?' I asked, seizing
my chance as Mrs Robbins paused for breath.

'Well now, I saw Verena Saturday morning—and perhaps I shouldn't say this, but we had a bit of an argument
about the flowers for decorating the church. It was my turn
to do them, but Verena wanted to take over and fill the
church with her lupins. I wasn't having that, and I told her
straight. Sunday was a special day for me—my wedding
anniversary—and I wasn't having Verena pushing in with
her lupins. They make a fine show, I grant you that, but I
stood my ground, and in the end she gave in. She wasn't in
church on Sunday, and I thought she was still in a huff
about the lupins—and of course she might have been. Or

she might have been dead already. She wasn't at the Parish Meeting on Monday, and she wasn't at the coffee morning on Tuesday, but—well, perhaps I shouldn't say this, but nobody minded all that much, she was so pushy, you know, it was really much nicer without her, and we never thought . . . Oh dear, it has been a shock to everyone. And only last Sunday we had the parable about the rich man and "Thou fool, this night shall thy soul be required of thee . . ." And oh, Miss Astolat dear, perhaps I shouldn't say this, but—' and her voice dropped to a whisper—'*they say it was poison . . .*'

Mrs Robbins at last ran out of breath and I was able to thank her, ring off, and sort out the information she had given me.

Verena had been seen by Mrs Robbins on Saturday morning, when they had an argument. Darius had seen her on Saturday afternoon, when he took the trio from Crispin Wharf House to visit her. And apparently nobody had seen her alive after that.

I remembered Darius warning me to keep away from drug-traffickers—'not nice people to get mixed up with,' he said.

But if I was right in my suspicions, then *he* was a drug-trafficker himself. And so was Philippa. And so was Verena. She had drawn attention to herself by giving me all that money. And now she was dead.

Something dreadful had happened at King's Martlet that Saturday afternoon. And fool that I was, I hoped against hope that Darius had not been involved. I was prepared to face the fact that he was a drug-smuggler—but not, please not, a murderer. A nasty little voice whispered that anybody who dealt in illicit drugs was already a murderer, but I refused to listen.

I stood looking down at the telephone for a long time. The thought of telephoning Darius terrified me. But I *had* to know.

I was about to pick up the phone when another nasty little voice whispered in my ear.

'Suppose Darius was involved in Verena's death—and he knows that you know—what then? Do you want him to come round here? *Do you want to die like Verena?*'

'He doesn't know my address,' I said. 'And I'm listed in the phone book under my real name, not Astolat.'

'He can easily find your address,' said the voice. 'In Philippa's files—phone number, address, everything. He already knows that you live in Blackheath, and that you live alone—you told him so in the Reef Knot Garden. *Keep him away from here!*'

I went out to the phone-box at the end of the street and rang Darius at the Magpie Inn.

'Astolat!' he said. 'Where are you? Are you all right— you dashed off so quickly last night . . .'

'I—I felt a migraine coming on,' I said. 'Sorry about that, but once I get the warning signs I have to head for home in a hurry.'

'What warning signs?' he said.

'Oh, flashing lights, zigzag patterns in front of my eyes, and a splitting headache,' I said. (Which was true, but not of my hurried departure from Crispin Wharf House the previous night.)

'Are you sure you're all right now?' he asked. He sounded quite genuinely concerned.

'Yes, I'm fine,' I said.

'Where are you?' he asked.

I hardened my heart.

I looked out of the phone-box at the block of flats across the road—Beaulieu Court

'I'm on my way to Beaulieu for the weekend,' I said. 'I'm going to do some research at the Motor Museum for my new book.'

(The last weekend in August was hardly the best time to visit the Motor Museum with a view to doing some quiet research . . . I hoped Darius wouldn't think of that.)

'Listen,' I said, 'I'm in a phone-box and I'm calling on a phone-card and it may run out any minute. But I've got to ask you—it's about Verena Gadsden—'

'Astolat,' said Darius firmly, 'I cannot tell you anything about the woman. I saw her for a few minutes on Saturday afternoon—'

'*What happened on Saturday afternoon?*' I said. 'It's important, Darius, really it is.'

Darius gave an exaggerated sigh and spoke very slowly and clearly.

'I took Mary and Philippa and Julian to see Verena. She came out to the porch and welcomed everybody. The others went into the house with her. That was the only time I saw her.'

'What happened then?' I asked.

'I went off to visit my brother and his family,' he said. 'They live only a few miles away. We went to the gymkhana at Shalford, where my niece Catherine won a rosette and a silver cup, and became quite unbearable. Then I went back to King's Martlet, collected Mary and Philippa and Julian, and took them back to Bettesham for the show. I didn't see Verena again.'

'You didn't go into the house—or the garden?'

'No—I just sat in the car and hooted, and Mary and Philippa came out. Old Julian was already out by the porch waiting for me—he was in a terrible state of nerves.'

'What was he nervous about?'

'Philippa says he's always like that before he does a show. I'd no idea anyone with his experience would go through such a bad time. He's been an actor all his life—you wouldn't think he had to worry about nerves before a performance. Fancy having to go through all that every time he goes on stage . . .'

'What form did his nerves take?'

'He just kept saying the Lord's Prayer over and over

again—sometimes quite loud, sometimes just a whisper—
but over and over again, without a break. As soon as he
reached "Amen" he'd be off again with "Our Father". Gave
me the creeps.'

'Sounds very odd,' I said.

'And he was shivering,' said Darius. 'I noticed Mary kept
her arm round him all the time they were in the car going
back to Bettesham—she sat in the back and I had old
Philippa beside me. I thought Julian might have had a bit
of consideration for Mary—after all, she was going to take
part in the show, so she might have been feeling nervous
too.'

'What happened when you got to Bettesham Court?'

'Oh, I let them go in without me. I took a long time
parking the car—I was glad to get away from them. Then
I went into the Great Hall, and mingled with the audience,
and just before the performance began, old Philippa came
and sat beside me.'

'What was the show like?' I asked.

'It's not really my kind of thing, but it went down very
well. A bunch of musicians in fancy dress began to play,
and then Julian and Mary swept in like a pair of peacocks.'

'No sign of nerves?' I said.

'Not a bit,' he said. 'They stood at lecterns, one each side
of the stage, and they read poems and things about love—'

'Of course,' I said. 'The show's called *A Lover and his Lass*,
isn't it.'

'I think they both knew the poems off by heart and were
only pretending to read,' said Darius. 'Because most of
the time they looked at the audience, and not at their
books.'

'That's exactly what Philippa told me to do,' I said.

'And in between whiles the musicians played soulful stuff.
The audience lapped it up—mind you, they'd all been
lapping up drinks in the bar beforehand, so perhaps they
were in the right mood. And at the end, Mary and the

musicians stepped back into the darkness and Julian stood alone on the stage and read a poem that had all the women in tears—even old Philippa was crying, although she pretended afterwards that she'd been trying to stifle a cough . . .'

'What was the poem?' I asked. I couldn't imagine any poem strong enough to reduce Philippa to tears.

'Something about being in two minds over a marriage with an impediment,' said Darius. 'I couldn't make head nor tail of it, but it certainly touched a soft spot among the women.'

'"*True* minds",' I said. 'Not "*two* minds".'

And I quoted:

> 'Let me not to the marriage of true minds
> Admit impediment . . .'

'That's it!' said Darius. 'You know it?'

'It's one of the most famous love poems in the English language,' I said.

'Oh well, you're a romantic novelist, you'd know all about things like that,' said Darius.

I pulled myself together. I wasn't ringing Darius to talk about love poetry, although it was a nice thought.

'Darius,' I said. 'Verena Gadsden is dead. They think she died on Saturday. You—'

Beep-beep, beep-beep. My phone card had run out.

I hung up.

At least I knew now that Darius was not guilty of Verena's death. If, that is, he had been telling me the truth.

I hurried back to my flat and grabbed the King's Martlet *Sentinel*, riffling through the pages to see if I could find anything about a gymkhana at Shalford. If there was nothing, I told myself, it didn't necessarily mean that Darius was lying—after all, the affairs of Shalford might not be reported in the King's Martlet paper—but I'd feel happier if it was.

Yes—there it was. 'Gymkhana at Shalford'. I looked at the list of winners. No sign of any Catherine Underwood— but yes, there she was, among the juniors. A rosette and a silver cup. I felt strangely comforted. It was pleasant to picture Darius with a brother and sister-in-law and a young niece who bounced about on a Thelwell pony. A nice, normal family, far removed from the frightening world of Crispin Wharf House.

Well, I'd done what I could for him.

I'd told him about Verena's death.

And now I'd never see him again.

CHAPTER 14

THE WEB

Somehow the day must have passed. There was just one long terrible ache, and I was at the centre of it.

At first I just sat and stared at nothing. Then I stared at the big crystal bowl on the windowsill. There was a chip on the rim like a crescent moon—I'd never noticed it before, but now I stared at it with rigid intensity. As the afternoon sun moved round, it struck patterns of rainbows from the crystal and spilled them over the wall. The sun went in, taking the rainbows with it. Later on, the sun reappeared from behind the clouds and flung the rainbows up on to the ceiling. Then the rainbows faded, and all the colour drained from the room. A whole day had passed, and I hadn't even noticed.

I switched on the television and stared at it, just as I had stared at the crystal bowl. It was the early evening news programme, but for all I cared it might have been a test-

card. Faces appeared on the screen, mouthing and over-
acting ridiculously. There was a jumble of strangers,
pointing dramatically to scenes of devastation—a plane
crash, a fire, a war. I turned the sound down. I didn't want
to hear what these foolish people were chattering about.
They had nothing to say to me.

Then a face appeared that looked vaguely familiar. A
little old man was waving a walking-stick decorated with
red ribbons. He stretched out his left arm and moved the
stick across it as though he was playing a violin. Charlie
Spink, the Perky Pensioner! What could *he* possibly have
done to qualify for inclusion in a major news programme?
I turned the sound up.

The camera cut to a group of Old Age Pensioners at an
airport. They were all returning from a holiday in Spain.
They wore souvenir sombreros, they clutched gaudy bags
embroidered with the single word TORREMOLINOS, and one
of them was clacking a pair of castanets with more enthusiasm than expertise. And, like Charlie Spink, they all had
aluminium walking-sticks, elbow-crutches or zimmer
frames from the National Health Service.

I recalled Charlie's entry in the Agency's pink booklet—
he offered to tell OAP's how to make money and have a lot
of fun at the same time, or something like that. Clearly he
had been leading this group on holiday, and they'd been
having a lot of fun. Judging by the pictures on the screen,
they still *were* having a lot of fun. But how were they making
money? And why were they on prime time television?

The camera cut to a close shot of Charlie Spink. He
flourished his walking-stick and then leered at the camera.
'If anybody makes it worth my while,' he said, 'I'm prepared
to sing.'

Had he formed a choir, and were they about to burst into
song? They stood there, giggling and smirking and waving
at the camera like a bunch of schoolkids. A group of re-
porters and photographers surrounded Charlie, laughing

and joking with him. Then came a shot of some men in uniform. Customs Officers. Even *they* looked happy. Their spokesman was on camera now.

'Charlie Spink—cut-price holidays in Spain for Senior Citizens . . . this bunch came sailing through the Green gates as happy as Larry . . . nothing to declare . . . and then one fool tripped over his walking-stick and out came the condoms—'

Condoms? Did I hear right?

'—condoms filled with cannabis and stuffed up the frame —see those frames—they're all lightweight aluminium— and they're hollow—thousands of pounds' worth of cannabis in every one . . .'

The camera cut to the 'fool'. He was grinning as he re-enacted the scene, tripping over his aluminium walking-stick and knocking off the rubber foot, and then pulling out a condom hidden inside the hollow stick. But—but the 'fool' was the Rabbit! And the man beside him was Mr Um!

The camera moved in closer and showed a rip in the condom. White powder was trickling out and blowing away. Nobody seemed to care that the stuff was as expensive as gold dust . . .

The lady with the castanets was egging on some of her friends to do some flamenco dancing. There were cries of '*Ole!*' and a lot of stamping, hand-clapping and finger-snapping. The film editor, who by now had got into the spirit of the thing, slapped a rip-roaring performance of *Carmen* on the sound-track. One of the fattest of the old ladies flung her arms round a small press photographer and galumphed joyfully around with him. The flamenco turned into a general knees-up, and then into the hokey-cokey. The dancers surged hand in hand towards the camera. It rocked, and the screen went blank.

I took off my hat to Charlie Spink. He'd brought a lot of fun into people's lives, just as he'd promised.

Slowly my mind clambered out of the deep freeze where

it had been all day. Little star-bursts appeared in the darkness of my head.

If Charlie Spink was smuggling cannabis, he had to be doing it for the Crispin Speakers' Agency.

And that meant that *Darius was innocent*!

I felt myself soaring through the ceiling.

I had to contact Darius, had to let him know—I had no idea what I was going to say, but the right words would surely come to me.

I dialled the Magpie Inn and asked for Darius.

The landlady answered. 'Mr Underwood's not here.'

I was checked, but not unduly bothered.

'Can you tell me when he'll be in?'

'He's gone for good,' she said.

The room swam. I heard her voice coming from a great distance.

'Packed up his things, paid his bill and left this morning. Had a phone call, and he was off. No, he didn't leave no forwarding address.' Her voice softened slightly and she added, 'Sorry, ducks.'

Then she rang off.

I stood staring at the telephone in my hand. Darius had received a phone call this morning. That must have been mine, telling him about Verena's death. Then he had packed up, paid his bill and disappeared. *He'd run away*. But—why?

He wasn't involved in the drugs racket.

He wasn't involved in Verena's death.

But he'd gone.

Somehow I had to find him, to tell him that everything was all right.

I must have been quite light-headed. My hair was untidy, my face was smudged with tears, I was wearing the old T-shirt and pants I'd been wearing all day, and I'd had nothing to eat or drink since breakfast, but I had no time to think of food or clothes. No time to think of anything but the absolute imperative of finding Darius.

But—where was he?

If he'd gone to Crispin Wharf House . . . I wasn't going inside there, not even for Darius. My blood ran cold at the thought of having to face Julian and Mary, or even worse, Philippa.

Yet I felt sure that he was somewhere around there, and that I should find him.

Then I thought of the one place where he might be hiding —on board the *Silver Swan*—in the narrow channel beside Crispin Wharf House, the channel masked by a curtain of greenery.

I couldn't wait for a bus. I half ran, half walked, all the way from Blackheath to Rotherhithe, and when I reached the main road I took the long way round to Crispin Wharf Street. I couldn't face the short cut through Magpie Lane. Some instinct, or perhaps it was my guardian angel, warned me against passing the Reef Knot Garden at night. It wasn't dark yet—it probably wouldn't get completely dark all night at this time of year—but it was twilight, and difficult to see things clearly, and there were no street lights in the lane. In short, I talked myself into going round by the road. The street lights were on here, yellow against the pale green of the summer evening, but the whole place seemed dead. The offices and shops were all shut up and padlocked, and there was hardly any traffic. I reached the dry-cleaners— closed but with a ghostly mauve fluorescent light somewhere inside—and turned the corner into Crispin Wharf Street. And there, at the far end, waiting for me, was Crispin Wharf House.

It was many months since I'd walked down Crispin Wharf Street—I'd always used the short cut through Magpie Lane —and I was unprepared for the changes there. The old derelict buildings had been demolished, and the open space behind the chain-link fencing was open no more. In their place, on either side of the street, were rows of bright new

terrace houses, each with a big FOR SALE notice in the
window.

The new houses cast a deep shadow across the pavement,
providing me with a welcome amount of cover. I felt like an
alley-cat, slipping along in the shadows, keeping close to
the walls, and all the time getting closer and closer to Crispin
Wharf House. Was there anybody inside it, and if so, were
they watching me, unseen?

I reached the end of the terrace and paused in the
shadows. Over to my right was the entrance to Magpie
Lane, grey and gloomy. Straight ahead of me was Crispin
Wharf House and the curtain of greenery stretching to the
builders' yard on the left. And behind the green curtain was
the narrow channel, and the *Silver Swan*—and Darius.

I stared at the windows of Crispin Wharf House, trying
desperately to see if anybody was looking out at me, but
there was no sign of life, and no sound. I screwed up my
courage and darted across the road.

The scent of spices came to meet me. I brushed against
the wall of the house and slid through the curtain of creepers,
heavy now with summer growth.

The channel was empty.

In the pale green light that filtered through the leaves I
could see the waters of the Thames flowing past at the far
end of the channel, and I could see the weed-covered timbers
of the landing-stage attached to Crispin Wharf House, hung
with swags of heavy mooring-chains and frayed rope fenders.
The walls on either side were streaked with green, and at
my feet were shallow steps leading down into the water,
which had risen to cover all but the very top one. The
channel was deep and narrow, just big enough for a small
boat. But there was no boat. There was no Darius.

I had been so sure of finding him here!

It took me quite a few minutes to let the realization sink
in.

On the far side of the channel was the high brick wall of

the builders' yard with its heavily padlocked gate. Could Darius possibly be hiding inside the yard? I moved carefully past the steps and tapped on the wooden gate.

'Darius,' I whispered. 'It's me, Astolat. Are you all right?'

There was no response. I waited for several minutes, and then tried again.

'Darius? Darius? It's me, Astolat . . .'

Still no response.

I stood with my back against the wall of the yard, pressing my hand against the hard rough surface of the bricks, as though physical pain would drive out the feeling of utter desolation that had taken hold of me. The only sound came from the water lapping gently against the steps. I stood staring down at it.

After a while I noticed that the water was lapping less gently. It was splashing up and over the top step. Something was moving in the river.

A couple of dinghies sailed past the end of the channel, tacking to make the most of the light breeze, and the heavy black barges moored in midstream rocked sedately. I caught sight of a flicker of white at the end of the channel, over to the right near the Crispin Wharf House landing-stage. Could it be the *Silver Swan* dancing in the wash of the dinghies?

I waited, but there was no more movement.

I could see no more of the landing-stage than the wooden piles alongside the mouth of the channel. The only way to see if the *Silver Swan* was moored in front of the landing-stage was to go past the front of Crispin Wharf House and then down the little alley on the far side.

And if the *Silver Swan* was *not* there?

I refused to think of that.

Quietly, and very, very cautiously, holding my breath, I went back through the curtain of creepers. I paused for a moment, straining to see if there was any movement in

Crispin Wharf Street or Magpie Lane, but all was still and silent. I flattened myself against the wall of Crispin Wharf House and inched my way along, bending double to pass below the level of the unlit windows, expecting every moment that a light would be switched on and that I should be discovered. At last I slipped thankfully into the shelter of the little alley. Something caught at my hair, and I was startled, but it was only the long fingers of the honeysuckle, and I shook myself free. I began to creep down the alley towards the landing-stage, keeping flat against the wall of the house and all the time edging towards the river, pausing, watching, listening.

I reached the little gate. Would it be locked? I tried it gently. It opened without a sound, and in a flash I was through it and on to the small square landing-stage, pressing myself back into the shadow of the house.

And there was the *Silver Swan*, riding easily at her moorings, not ten feet away from me. As I watched, she dipped up and down once or twice, as though somebody was moving about on board.

Darius?

Hardly daring to breathe, with my heart thumping and my blood pounding in my ears, I moved cautiously, a step at a time, towards the *Silver Swan*.

I was half way across the landing-stage, almost within touching distance of the boat, when a lamp was suddenly switched on downstairs, sending light flooding out through the windows and catching me in its beam.

I froze.

'Mary *darling*—is that you?'

It was Julian's voice.

I remembered Darius's description of Julian at King's Martlet, repeating the Lord's Prayer over and over again without a pause. Had he been trying to blot out the memory of what had happened to Verena earlier that afternoon—if it *had* happened then?

Now Julian was standing by the open french windows, and was looking directly at me.

I was trapped.

I'd have to try to bluff my way out.

'It's all right, Julian,' I shouted. 'It's me—Astolat!'

If Darius was on board, he'd hear that, and if Julian dragged me into the house, Darius would come to my rescue.

Julian smiled.

'Astolat! Elaine, the lily maid! Come in, darling, come in!'

('"Will you walk into my parlour?" said the spider to the fly . . .')

Taking a deep breath, and cursing herself for a fool, the fly walked in.

CHAPTER 15

TIME'S FOOL

'*Darling* Astolat, you've saved my *life*!' cried Julian. 'Mary's at the studios, Philippa's disappeared, and I can't get this *idiotic* machine to work. I'm sure *you* know how to do it . . .'

If he was a spider, he was a remarkably relaxed one. He was wearing an elegant silk shirt and slacks and Italian sandals, and he had a glass of whisky in his hand. He gestured towards a portable tape-recorder standing on the glass-topped table. I approached it carefully. It didn't look like a trap . . .

Then, beyond the pool of light in which we stood, somebody moved towards me from the far end of the room.

'Who's that?' I cried, and realized almost immediately that it was my own reflection in one of the long wall mirrors.

'That,' said Julian, 'is a *charming* young lady called Astolat who is about to work some magic on this machine . . . Ah,

what it is to be young . . . I can't see to read the symbols
on the tape-recorder without my reading glasses, and even
with my glasses I don't understand what all those arrows
and thingies mean . . .'

'Do you want Playback or Record? 'I asked, as I switched
on the power.

'Oh, Playback,' said Julian.

'What's it a recording of?' I asked.

'It's a tape of *A Lover and his Lass*—we did it at Danesborough last night, and I made a few changes to my delivery
of the opening poem.'

I pressed the Playback switch.

A high, sweet pipe traced the melody of the opening
music—Arne's setting of 'It was a Lover and his Lass'.
Other instruments joined in. I kept my eye upon Julian.

'*Wonderful* girl!' he said. 'I *knew* you could do it. Let me
get you a drink.'

I looked at the gilded trolley with its decanters and
ice-bucket and all the paraphernalia of a well-stocked bar,
including an impressive array of Dartington glass. Nice,
heavy lead crystal. Just what I needed.

'Plain tonic water, please,' I said.

It would be difficult for him to introduce poison into a
tonic bottle while I was watching. (I remembered Mrs
Robbins whispering down the phone, '*They say it was
poison . . .*')

Julian's hand hovered over the glasses. I hefted a tumbler,
held it out to him, and he filled it with tonic water.

'Ice?' he said, smiling, and I shook my head.

I'd already satisfied myself that the heavy tumbler was
completely clean and empty. If I *had* to drink from it, it
seemed safe enough. And if he threatened me with violence
I hoped I should be able to use it as a weapon and stun him
with it. Not perhaps the usual way to approach a social
drink, but some of the Borgias' dinner-guests might have
done well to adopt a similarly cautious view.

He led me over to the couch and we sat down.

On the tape the music ended, and Julian's voice took over.

> Come live with me and be my love
> And we will all the pleasures prove . . .

It was the voice of a young man in the prime of his life, pretending to coax, but all the time supremely confident of getting his way with the little shepherdess. For the first time I realized that the old man sitting beside me had once been a gorgeous *young* man. I was tempted to close my eyes and let the beautiful, seductive voice wash over me. Then I thought of that same beautiful voice endlessly repeating the Lord's Prayer at King's Martlet, and I kept my eyes firmly open.

Julian seemed to have forgotten all about me. He was sitting absolutely still, listening intently, frowning slightly, his eyes closed.

The poem came to a close.

> If these delights thy mind may move,
> Then live with me and be my Love.

There was a moment's silence, and then Julian sighed and came out of his trance.

'Right, you can switch off now,' he said.

'That was lovely, Julian,' I said, and I meant it. I'd been surprised to find him worrying about his performance. I'd rather assumed that he would rely on his beautiful voice to float him over everything.

'I think on the *whole* it was pretty good,' he said. 'There are one or two little things that can be improved. I'll do it better next time . . .'

I went over to the recorder, and as I put out my hand to switch it off, a thought struck me. I switched from Playback to Record, and hoped that the little built-in microphone would pick up our voices. If anything nasty happened to me, I wanted to leave a witness.

Julian showed no interest in my manœuvres with the tape-recorder. He wasn't even looking at it. Perhaps he was still brooding about the 'little things' that he'd do better next time.

I picked up my glass and sat down beside him on the pale leather couch. It was placed across the middle of the room with its back to the windows, making a big self-contained reception area, quite separate from Philippa's office over by the french windows. I could see the spiral staircase reflected in one of the wall mirrors, and I could also see the reflection of the *Silver Swan* moored outside at the little landing-stage. But if Darius left the boat and looked through the windows he wouldn't be able to see me sitting on the far side of the low couch, because my head didn't reach the top. Julian, of course, was so tall that his auburn hair would show up high above the back of the couch.

I raised the tumbler to my lips, but didn't actually drink from it.

'Julian,' I said, 'what happened at King's Martlet last Saturday?'

He looked surprised.

'*Nothing* happened at King's Martlet,' he said. 'The show was at Bettesham Court—it was part of the Bettesham Festival. Mary and I have a *tremendous* following there still. Quite touching. And it went down very well. *Marvellous* atmosphere . . .'

'I mean—before you gave the show—didn't you go to King's Martlet to see Verena Gadsden?'

'Oh yes. Stupid idea. We should never have gone there. I needed peace and quiet for my ritual—you see, before every show I have to recite the Lord's Prayer continually —mustn't stop or something terrible will happen.' (He sounded a bit like the Lady of Shalott . . .) 'I recite the Lord's Prayer—I set out my make-up—I check my costume —I do my breathing exercises—I keep on saying the Lord's Prayer—I step on to the stage with my *left* foot—that's *very* important—'

'But what happened to Verena?' I said.

'I've no idea,' he said. 'Stupid woman. Never stopped chattering. I could have *killed* her.'

He seemed quite unaware of what he had just said.

'And did you?' I said. (Perhaps shock tactics would work.)

'Did I what?'

'Did you kill Verena?'

'No, of course I didn't. I left her with Philippa and Mary and I went round to the front of the house and waited for Darius to come back in the car.'

'Did you have to wait long?' I asked.

'Oh, *hours*,' said Julian. 'Hours and hours and *hours* . . .'

Julian wasn't making much of a witness.

'Can you remember if Philippa said anything to Verena about cannabis?'

'Why the devil should she do that?' He seemed genuinely surprised.

I took a deep breath and plunged in.

'Because Verena was buying cannabis from some of the Crispin Agency speakers, and Philippa was organizing the whole thing.'

Julian laughed and put down his empty glass.

'Astolat darling, forgive me—but *really*—your novelist's imagination has run away with you! What absolute nonsense!'

'No, Julian!'

It was Philippa's voice.

She was coming down the spiral staircase behind us. I could see her reflection in one of the wall mirrors.

I wondered how much of our conversation she had overheard, and I took a firmer grasp upon the heavy tumbler.

It was my only weapon. If it failed me, and I had to make a quick exit, I would try to dart round the couch and make for the french windows, the landing-stage, the *Silver Swan* and—I hoped—Darius.

'It's quite true, Julian,' said Philippa.

She came down the stairs, and I saw that she was wearing a sweater and pants and carrying an overnight bag. Philippa was going to cut and run for it. She didn't look at me. Her eyes were fixed upon Julian as he rose to his feet and went towards her.

I huddled down into my corner and tried to make myself invisible as I watched them in the mirrors.

'They've caught Charlie Spink,' she said. 'I saw him on the telly. He won't be keeping his mouth shut.'

'What the hell has Charlie Spink got to do with it?' he said.

'Listen, Julian,' she said. 'I asked Darius to bring the *Silver Swan* to the landing-stage and make sure that she had enough fuel for a long journey. The boat's out there now, waiting for us. We've still got time to get away. We can do it . . . Just grab some clothes and any money you can lay your hands on and come with me.'

Julian stood very still.

'*I* give the orders in this house, Philippa,' he said coldly. '*I* am in charge of the Agency, and *I* am responsible for the organization.'

'The only time *you* did any organizing you nearly wrecked the entire operation,' said Philippa viciously. 'February 14th—St Valentine's Day—remember?'

'Of *course* I remember,' said Julian angrily. 'You were away for the day. The wretched Contessa let us down at the last moment, and *I* had to get somebody to deputize for her at a *minute's* notice. I flatter myself I organized the whole thing extremely well.'

'You did not,' said Philippa.

'The booker,' said Julian, 'had engaged a romantic

novelist to give a talk on St Valentine's Day. The Contessa let us down, and I sent *another* romantic novelist to take her place. I sent Elaine Astolat.'

'She stuck you for a first-class ticket, *and* a taxi all the way out to Blackheath,' said Philippa.

'She was doing us a *favour*,' said Julian.

(So I was too . . . but this was no time for me to draw attention to myself.)

'Since when do speakers do us a favour by accepting extra engagements that we get for them?' said Philippa. 'And you didn't have the sense to tell me about the change-over until it was too late for me to do anything.'

'It was *all* in *hand*,' said Julian. 'There was *nothing* for you to do.'

'Oh yes there was,' said Philippa. 'The Contessa was supposed to be carrying a supply of cannabis with her—she used to conceal it in a plastic envelope under the dust-jacket of a book—and two distributors were going to the meeting to buy it from her.'

'The Contessa!' said Julian.

'Your clever change-over meant that the distributors mistook Astolat for the Contessa, and when she refused to sell them her book, they followed her on to the train and pinched her bag with the book in it. She stopped the train and they had to run for it. They got the book—found nothing inside it—oh, they did find and destroy a Polaroid photograph that might have interested the police—and the next day they called here—and *I* was the one who had to deal with them. I had to hand over a whole lot of cannabis —otherwise they'd have broken the place up.'

'The Contessa!' said Julian. 'That little fool? She's been carrying cannabis for *you*?'

'She's one of my regulars,' said Philippa. 'The excitement gives her a buzz. Besides, she's always short of money . . .'

'Who else is in it?' said Julian.

'Chris the candle-maker—hides his supply in the base of

one of his candles. And there's old Gussie Greenfingers with her pot plants—more pot than plant sometimes . . .'

'And who brings it into the country?'

'Charlie Spink. He and his bunch of pensioners brought a cartload in with them on this last trip, but some silly fool gave the game away at the airport and Customs nabbed the lot. Well, it's every man for himself now!'

They had both forgotten me. They were standing between the couch and the windows in a pool of light, like actors upon a stage. I was hidden from them by the back of the couch, but if they glanced in any of the mirrors they might see my reflection. Luckily most of the mirrors were in shadow. I sat very still, making myself as small as possible in the corner of the couch, and never loosening my grasp of the tumbler.

'I haven't got much money with me,' said Philippa. 'But I've got plenty of cannabis, *and* I've got some of the hard stuff. I can find a market for it wherever we go—it's a universal currency.'

'But Philippa, *why*? In God's name, *why* have you been doing this?'

She took a deep breath.

'I did it for you, Julian. You needed beautiful things around you—you wouldn't be *you* without them. But they cost money—the *Silver Swan*—and all this . . .' Her gesture took in the whole of Crispin Wharf House and its luxurious lifestyle.

'Philippa *darling*, I have always been *perfectly* capable of supporting my wife and myself—*and* paying your salary!' He almost spat the words at her, but she was unmoved.

'No, Julian. *I* have supported all three of us for years on the cannabis operation. The amount of money you bring in from your acting jobs wouldn't keep you in Gucci loafers!'

The blow went home. Julian's face was chalk-white, and for a moment I thought he was going to faint. Philippa saw it too, and her expression softened. Then, to my astonishment, she put her arms around him.

'Oh Julian, I'm sorry it's turned out like this,' she said. 'I meant everything for the best. I have kept faith with you. I haven't forgotten our wonderful weekend together, my dear.' (I pricked up my ears at this. Julian—and *Philippa?*) 'You were the star of Bettesham Rep, and I was just a scruffy little Assistant Stage Manager, seventeen years old and a nobody. I wasn't even pretty. But you took me to a little inn beside the river . . .' (It didn't need a novelist's imagination to guess that Julian had taken many other girls to the little inn beside the river.) 'You said we could never be married, because of Mary, but that ours would be a marriage of the mind.' (He'd said that to many other girls too.) 'And then you read me the sonnet that begins:

>"Let me not to the marriage of true minds
>Admit impediment . . ."'

The very lines that Philippa had suggested to me as an ending for my talk on Romantic Novelists! Quite a lot of things were beginning to make sense now. Poor old Philippa! I'd have thought her the very last person to be swept off her feet by a passionate one night stand. But she had hugged that memory to her for something like thirty years. (Thirty years! I wasn't even born then . . .) I tried to think myself back into the 'fifties, when Philippa was seventeen, when romance was *Brief Encounter*, with Celia Johnson saying goodbye to Trevor Howard on a railway station. After Philippa's weekend with the star of Bettesham Rep she had settled for a life as a hard-working dogsbody in a theatre where she'd be unlikely to meet any man to rival Julian. When the theatre closed, she had jumped at the chance to follow Julian and Mary to their new home in Rotherhithe, and she had spent fifteen years as the mainstay of the Crispin Speakers' Agency. What was more, she had even made herself believe all that waffle about a marriage of the mind. Beneath her armour-plating of cool common sense, Philippa Preston was a thoroughgoing Romantic.

And Julian? I guessed that he took her devotion as his due, and if he thought of her at all, regarded her as a useful piece of furniture, as solid and as unremarkable as her big desk by the french windows.

I shifted my position slightly to get a better view of them in another mirror. I could see Philippa's face more clearly now. The radiance of her smile transformed her, so that she looked almost beautiful.

'Last Saturday,' she said, 'at Bettesham Court, you spoke the same lines, and I knew that you were remembering that weekend all those years ago:

"Love's not Time's fool, though rosy lips and cheeks
Within his bending sickle's compass come . . ."

When you said those words, you looked straight at me, and I knew then that you have always loved me—just as I have always loved you.'

Her voice cracked, and she brushed away the tears. ('All the women were in tears,' Darius had said. 'Even old Philippa.')

'Don't be *ridiculous*, Philippa!' said Julian pettishly. He pulled himself free of her. 'I didn't look at *anybody* when I spoke the sonnet. I was wearing my *reading-glasses*. I couldn't see *anything* beyond the lectern. I didn't even know you were in the audience. I might just as well have been speaking to a sack of potatoes.'

The fool! The stupid, self-centred fool!

With those cruel words he killed her as surely as if he had plunged a knife into her heart.

And he didn't even realize he'd done it.

As I watched her in the mirror, she staggered and seemed to shrivel, like a balloon when the party's over and the guests have gone. Her arms dropped limply to her sides and her mouth went slack.

She stood staring at him for a long time, and I was shocked at the empty look in her eyes.

At last she said slowly, 'What a fool I've been all these years . . . what a silly, trusting *fool*.'

She clamped a hand over her mouth. Philippa despised weakness in herself even more than in others. She looked at Julian very hard, and then she lifted her chin.

'For the first time in thirty years I'm seeing you as you really are . . . and you're just—a nobody. Goodbye, Julian. I'll go it alone.'

She picked up her bag, turned towards the french windows, thrust aside the long curtains and ran out on to the little landing-stage.

Julian started to follow her, then paused in the open doorway and watched her go. In three strides she had crossed the landing-stage and reached the boat.

I crept quietly towards the tape-recorder. All I had to do now was to grab it and run while Julian had his back to me and all his attention was centred on Philippa.

Looking through the window, I saw her jump on to the deck and go below.

Then there was an appalling explosion and the *Silver Swan* blew up.

A blinding white light filled the room, and there was a terrible roaring all around me. Perhaps it only lasted a few seconds, but it seemed like eternity.

I could hear myself screaming, yet inside I was praying that Darius might be safe somehow, somewhere . . .

In the doorway, Julian spun round towards me, his body rigid, his face a mask of terror.

Flames from the *Silver Swan* shot across the little landing-stage and clawed at his back.

For a moment I saw him standing there, black against the background of flames, his head thrown back, his hair a

halo of fire. His clothes were ablaze, and flames were streaming out of him.

With a snap like a rifle shot, the mirror cracked from side
to side.

The curtains flew outwards, sucked back by the blast.

Julian cried out, stretching his arms towards me, but he
too was sucked backwards until he vanished into the roaring
mass of flames. Where he had been standing there was
nothing but a hole in the air and, in the background, a wall
of fire.

The same immense force reached out for me, drew me
across the room, and hurled me into blackness.

CHAPTER 16

EDGE OF DOOM

When I came to a few seconds later I found myself lying
huddled against the side of Philippa's big desk in a thick
red fog of choking dust. There was a roaring in my ears and
a terrible tightness in my chest as I fought to raise my head
above the fog. The desk had shielded me from the worst of
the blast, but I had to get away fast before the house caught
fire.

Gradually the dust settled. The lights had all gone out,
but the red glare from the burning boat showed me that the
timbers supporting the ceiling were standing firm. Most of
the furniture had been tossed around and toppled over,
the drinks trolley lay smashed and the elegant lamps had
collapsed. There seemed to be a lot of broken glass everywhere, and I could hear more glass tinkling down from the
windows.

The floor was hot to my touch as I crawled on hands and
knees, pushing aside the heavy furniture, cutting myself on

broken glass, but all the time making for the main door.

I felt a stream of cool air and headed towards it. The door was open just a crack. I pulled it open, crawled through and found myself in the side alley.

I sat with my back against the alley wall, coughing and retching and then drawing some fresh air down into my lungs. I tried to haul myself up by clinging to the bines of honeysuckle, but they crumbled into tinder as I touched them.

I crawled out of the alley into the street and there, slowly, still hanging on to the alley wall, I pulled myself up to my feet. My legs were trembling and my heart was pounding, and now for the first time I realized that I was still clutching the tape-recorder. I felt sure that it was important, but I couldn't remember why.

I looked up. The flames from the boat were leaping high in the air, higher than the house, and above the flames, thick black smoke rolled and climbed to the sky.

A roar from within the building told me that the current of air from the open door had swept through the room towards the open windows, and that the whole of the ground floor of Crispin Wharf House was burning. In a matter of minutes, the whole house would be ablaze. Then the flames would reach out to the new terrace houses, standing empty with their FOR SALE notices, and to the old warehouses in Magpie Lane. They too would be empty at this time on a Saturday night. But at the far end of Magpie Lane was the Magpie Inn, and people would be sleeping there. I must rouse them and use their phone to call the Fire Brigade.

I plunged into Magpie Lane. It was dark between the tall old buildings. Here and there a narrow alleyway on the left glowed red from the river. Then all was dark again.

I tried to force myself to run, but my legs seemed to be made of rubber. There was no sound apart from the roaring of the fire, and no light apart from the flames. No house lights, no street lamps, no voices. Magpie Lane might have been a street of the dead.

The blazing boat itself was hidden from me by the riverside warehouses, but the red light was reflected on the upper storeys of the buildings, and the flames threw giant shadows high above me.

There was a whoosh and a roar and a crash. Crispin Wharf House had fallen in upon itself. Flames leaped up, and the shadows leaped with them.

I ran, staggered and fell, tripping on the uneven paving stones, picking myself up and making myself run on. I must be getting near to the end of the lane. The Magpie Inn was just ahead . . .

I stopped.

There was a flood of red light across my path.

I had come to the open space of the Reef Knot Garden. The glare from the burning boat had spread all over the river. The wharves and warehouses on the opposite bank were red, their windows flaring as though they too were on fire. The barges moored in midstream, the rusty old hulks lying downstream, all were red. The air was full of flying debris, showers of glittering dust and sparks that flared up and died. At the topmost level of the Garden, the three reef knots reared up black against the red sky. And high above everything the black smoke billowed and grew.

I could not—I simply could *not*—walk forward alone and unprotected past that open space. But I had to reach the Magpie Inn. I *had* to pass the Reef Knot Garden.

'Magpie Inn!' I said to myself. 'Magpie, phone, Fire Brigade. Magpie, phone, Fire Brigade. Magpie, phone, Fire Brigade . . .'

I braced myself and stepped into the red glare.

'Magpie, phone—'

'Help!'

A faint cry stopped me.

'Astolat—help me!'

The voice was too faint for me to identify, but there was only one person that it could be.

Darius!

He was somewhere inside the Reef Knot Garden, and he needed my help.

'Hold on!' I cried. 'Hold on, Darius . . . I'm coming . . . it's me, Astolat . . .'

And I stepped into the shadowy Garden.

To the left of the entrance was the fallen red oil drum, still supporting the twisted cables that looked like a skein of wool with a knitting needle thrust through it. The iron bar of the 'knitting needle' seemed to be balanced very precariously and I was picking my way past it very carefully when something fell to the ground with a clatter. The tape-recorder. Well, it could stay there. I wasn't going to need it.

I looked around. As far as I could tell in the uncertain flickering light, there was no sign of Darius at ground level.

I started cautiously up the first flight of steps.

Above me, to the left of the trio of reef knots, something moved and then was still. That was the point I had to aim for. The steps, of course, led me away to the right.

I started up the next flight of steps and missed my footing, landing on hands and knees, cursing the architect who had designed the crazy pattern of zigzagging steps and ramps and walkways. It might be amusing by daylight, but it was not funny now. I picked myself up, found the next bit of zigzag and went up it carefully, my eyes fixed on the steps. It would be time enough to look around for Darius when I reached the topmost tier. As I got there I stumbled again, and to save myself from falling I put out my right hand and caught hold of the right-hand reef knot.

At that moment someone grasped me from behind and forced me up and nearly over the low brick wall into the Thames. Only my grip on the reef knot saved me from going right over and into the water. The dank river smell was all around me, and bits of wood and plastic debris raced by at a terrifying speed. The river was running faster than I had ever seen it. Was it high tide? Ebb tide? I didn't know. I only knew that the water was almost within touching distance. How deep was it here? 'About as high as a house,' Darius had said. I wasn't going down there.

After the first shock of fear at seeing the water so close to me, I felt nothing but sheer boiling rage. It was humiliating to find myself in such a ridiculous position, head down and spreadeagled over the wall, but I was *not* going to be heaved ignominiously into the Thames like a bucket of bilge water.

I hung grimly on to the reef knot. The rough bristles of the twisted rope bit into my hand, but I hung on. The iron rod that ran through the cable was embedded deep in concrete, and it wouldn't let me down. I hooked my right foot around the base of the reef knot, jamming it down savagely between the cable and the brick wall. My attacker would have a job to move me now.

And he was beginning to tire. He had lost the advantage of surprise, and his grip on me was weakening. I could hear him breathing hard as he tried once more to force me into the river.

I managed to get my left hand behind my back, felt blindly for the top of the wall, and clutched at it. Then I levered myself up and back, and found myself suddenly upright once more, still gripping the reef knot with my right hand.

My attacker fell back with a grunt, and I swung myself round to face him.

He was a small, bald-headed man in a track suit.

I stared at him in amazement. I don't know what I had expected to see, but this was not it.

A brilliant shower of sparks sputtered past overhead, and by their light I saw a large amethyst ring on his right hand. I recognized that ring, and at that moment I recognized its wearer.

Mary Michaelmas.

Mary Michaelmas, without her wig of pretty silvery curls, her real hair so thin that she looked bald in the dim red light. Mary Michaelmas in an old track suit.

She smiled and touched the ring. A tiny needle shot out.

I knew then.

I didn't understand, but I *knew*. One scratch from that needle, and I was done for.

I tried to turn and run, but my right foot was still jammed between the reef knot and the wall. The very thing that had saved my life was going to be my death-trap.

I struggled desperately to free myself, all the time keeping my eyes fixed on Mary as she came slowly towards me along the narrow walkway. She stretched out her left hand, ready to grab my wrist and plunge in the needle.

I kicked out sharply with my left foot and caught her on the shinbone.

She staggered backwards. Her right hand flew up, the amethyst ring struck her neck, and the needle went home.

She gave a hoarse cry and clawed frantically at her throat, trying to pull the needle out.

Her arms flailed in the air as she lost her balance and fell forward, toppling off the walkway and rolling down and down the zigzag of steps and ramps until she reached ground level and crashed into the fallen oil drum.

I couldn't see exactly what happened next, although I could hear the drum rolling away into the road. Perhaps the movement of the drum disturbed the precarious balance of the 'knitting needle', perhaps Mary grabbed at it and pulled it down upon herself. I saw her fall backwards, her arms flung wide, and I saw the heavy iron bar fall across her, pinning her to the ground.

Now that the immediate danger was over, my right foot unjammed itself from the reef knot with the greatest of ease. It hurt damnably, and so did my ribs from being pressed

against the wall. But at least I was mobile again now, and
Mary, thank God, was not.

'Help me!' she cried. 'Help me, Astolat!'

I limped painfully down the steps towards her. There was
nothing I could do to help. A long time ago Darius and I
had tried to lift one of the cables with the iron centres and
had found it too heavy. Besides, I had no illusions about
Mary. She had tried to kill me, and even now, close to death
as she was, she would take me with her if she got the chance.
So I kept my distance.

I looked at the scratch on her throat, and I looked at the
amethyst ring with its deadly needle.

'A poison ring!' I said. 'I thought that sort of thing went
out with the Borgias.'

'I didn't know it was a poison ring,' said Mary. She
sounded like a petulant child. 'I bought it in an antique
shop and I just wore it because I liked it. Then one day—
by chance—I touched the spring and discovered the needle.
I used it on Bunty Beresford at the Royal Casterbridge . . .'

A shudder went through her, and I guessed that the
poison had started to work.

I began to piece things together.

'Bunty Beresford!' I said. 'I thought *Verena* had poisoned
her! But I remember now . . . *I actually saw you patting Bunty's
hand at the Royal Casterbridge reception.* I thought you were
trying to help her—but you were killing her with that
damned ring!'

'Yes, I was killing her,' said Mary. 'I had to get rid of
her—she guessed too much.' She smiled. 'But she never
guessed that I was running the organization.'

'You!' I said. 'I thought it was Philippa!'

'Philippa does the routine stuff, but I do the masterminding,' said Mary. '*I* set up the Crispin Speakers' Agency, and
later on *I* set up the cannabis operation . . .'

'How did it start?' I asked.

'It started,' said Mary, 'with Bamba.'

'Bamba?' I said. 'Madame Bamba, the dress woman?'

I saw again the heavy body in the black dress, the blood-red nails, the white face, and the black beehive of hair.

Mary nodded.

'She's got a couple of dress shops, and a nightclub called The Spider's Web—that's a good name—most of her agents are flies who got trapped in her web—just as I did.'

'What happened?' I asked.

'I went to buy—' she coughed, and then went on—'I went to buy a dress at Bambinetta—I often went there— but one day she kept me waiting a long time, and I was furious. She'd got some jewellery on display, and there was nobody at Reception, so I thought I'd pay her out for keeping me waiting, and I slipped a brooch into my bag— and at that moment—'

'At that moment,' I said, 'Madame Bamba stepped out of the lift and caught you?'

Many things were becoming clearer to me now.

Mary nodded.

'Bamba the mamba,' she said. 'That's when she started to squeeze me—quite gently at first. Then I bought a dress I couldn't pay for, and she offered me—'

'Facilities?' I said.

She nodded again.

'My father had a saying, "Take what you want, says God, take what you want—and pay for it." Madame Bamba has the same idea—especially the bit about paying. Easy payments—only they weren't so easy . . .'

Her lips drew back in a painful attempt at a smile.

'Then she introduced me to her gambling club. At first I won quite a lot of money . . . but then I began to lose . . . and lose . . . and then she said she'd cancel all my debts if I'd carry cannabis for her.'

She closed her eyes for a moment.

'Well, that's how it started,' she said. 'I became one of

Bamba's distributors . . . she caught the Contessa the same way. The Contessa's a fool, she actually takes the stuff . . .'

No wonder the Contessa occasionally missed an engagement, like the one on St Valentine's Day.

'Then Bamba suggested that I should set up my own organization—as a branch of the Bamba network—using some of the people in the Crispin Speakers' Agency . . .'

'You do the organizing, your carriers run the risks, and Bamba sits back and takes a hefty rake-off?' I said.

'Yes,' said Mary. She sighed. 'And it worked very well until you turned up. We were moving into cocaine, and that means *real* money. I made a mistake when I brought you on to our books, Astolat. I thought all romantic novelists must be fools like the Contessa . . .'

Her voice tailed away, but she roused herself.

'Verena was a fool too,' she said viciously. 'Giving you all that money—oh yes, the faithful Philippa reported that to me. We went down to King's Martlet before we did the Bettesham show. I told Philippa to clear the cannabis out of the house while Verena and I went for a walk in the garden. We went for a walk in the garden and I killed her with my ring . . .'

Her voice was getting weaker, but I was not to be lured any closer.

'I'm not the dumbo people like to think I am,' she said. 'Poor old Philippa hasn't got half my brains. She thinks she's doing all this for Julian . . . poor thing, she's been in love with him for years, and he doesn't give a damn about her . . . Where is she now?'

I gestured towards the red glare from the burning boat.

'As soon as I saw Charlie Spink on television, I guessed Philippa would try to get away on the *Silver Swan*. I fixed things so that it would explode as soon as she turned on the engine . . .' She gave a high, cracked laugh. 'I was doing that when you suddenly appeared on the landing-stage and announced your arrival at the top of your voice . . .'

So it had been Mary moving about on the boat, not
Darius . . .

So—where was Darius? What had happened to him?

'Where's Julian?' she asked.

I recalled my last sight of Julian. I couldn't tell her that.
'Philippa . . . took him with her,' I said.

'Poor old Jule,' she said softly. 'We had some good times
together . . . He always needed money, but he didn't know
how to earn it.' She smiled faintly. 'He knew how to spend
it all right . . . we had some good times . . .'

She fell silent for a long while, and I thought her breathing
had stopped. Then she opened her eyes and smiled.

'Julian!' she said.

And then she died.

CHAPTER 17

JOURNEY'S END

Suddenly there were lights everywhere, and the whole river
sprang into life. Fire-fighting boats were heading for the
Silver Swan. I could hear the sirens of police cars and fire
engines coming nearer and nearer as they raced along the
main road towards Crispin Wharf House.

A boat with a powerful searchlight came racing upstream,
swung in towards the Reef Knot Garden and stopped. After
the dim red haze from the burning boat, the brilliance of
the searchlight blinded me, and I shut my eyes.

When I opened them again, a man was leaping down
from the boat-deck. He put out his hand and steadied
himself against one of the three reef knots and then jumped
down into the Garden.

The boat swung away again, and he was caught in the
beam of the searchlight.

It was Darius.

Darius, alive and unharmed.

I gave thanks silently.

The beam of the searchlight swung over the Reef Knot Garden as the boat moved away upstream again, and Darius saw me huddled on the ground. I tried to call out to him, but I couldn't make a sound.

The light from the boat disappeared, and Darius switched on a torch that cut through the red haze. He came leaping down the steps towards me.

I must have made a strange picture, my clothes torn and blackened by the explosion, my face smeared and dusty. I put up my hand to shield my eyes from the torch's beam.

'Astolat . . .?' he said.

He sounded as though he didn't believe what he saw.

Then he was on his knees beside me, and his arms were around me.

'Astolat! Darling, darling Astolat . . . oh my dear, dear girl!'

I buried my face in his shoulder and sobbed my heart out. He let me cry, holding me in his arms and murmuring my name over and over again.

At last he held me at arm's length and looked at me.

'Your hands are bleeding,' he said. 'How—'

'It's nothing,' I said. 'It's all right now . . .'

'You're sure?' he said.

'I'm . . . just tired . . . I want to go to sleep . . .'

I wanted to snuggle down into his arms again, but he shook me awake.

'For God's sake, Astolat, *what has happened here?*'

I gulped and tried to pull myself together.

'The *Silver Swan* blew up,' I said.

'I saw it,' he said. 'Where's Philippa?'

'She was on board,' I said. 'Julian died in the explosion too.'

'And Mary?'

'She's here,' I said.

I disengaged myself unwillingly from his arms and showed him where Mary lay. He rose and went towards her, swinging the torch's beam across her body.

'That's *Mary*?' he said incredulously.

The light caught the amethyst ring.

'Be careful, Darius!' I cried. 'It's a poison ring!'

'What happened?' he said.

'The poison needle caught her in the throat—she was trying to kill me with it but she fell . . .'

My voice was no more than a hoarse whisper. I didn't even know if he could hear me.

'She was trying to kill me . . .'

'It's all over now,' he said. 'Nobody will hurt you. Come along, I'll take you away.'

He put his arm around me and I stumbled past Mary's body. There was a sudden clatter as my foot kicked against something. Darius swung his torch over the ground.

'I'll be damned,' he said. 'It's a tape-recorder. Somebody must have dropped it in a hurry.'

'Oh, it's terribly important,' I said. 'At least . . . it was going to be terribly important, but I can't remember why . . .'

'Here,' he said. 'You take it. We'll find out if it's important later on.'

I clutched the recorder. I still couldn't think why it should be important to me, but I knew that it was.

The red glare was beginning to fade into the general dimness of the summer night. The fire at Crispin Wharf House must be under control. I felt curiously detached about it all, as though I was floating along on a cloud.

Later that night I really was floating—Darius and I were standing in a boat, and I could feel a cool breeze on my face. I looked up and saw Tower Bridge ahead of us. Then we passed underneath and came out on the other side. I didn't care where we were going. Darius had his arm around me, and that was all that mattered.

We were in a big building, walking down some long, empty corridors. There were only a few lights on, and the place was very quiet.

Then we were sitting in comfortable chairs in a big office, facing a tall, thin man with bright brown eyes and a grey moustache, like an old grey fox. I noticed that his office had a large desk and a lot of carpet. If this was a Government office, the grey fox must be one of the high-ups.

The tape-recorder stood on his desk. He and Darius sat quietly as I switched on the machine, ran it on Fast Rewind and then on Playback. When the shrill pipe began to play 'It Was a Lover and his Lass', the grey fox raised one eyebrow in my direction.

'This first bit is a recording of a show called *A Lover and his Lass*,' I said. 'Julian Leigh listened to it at Crispin Wharf House last night. Then he asked me to switch off the machine, but I switched it on to Record instead. I hope you'll be able to hear the conversation between Julian and Philippa Preston—they were talking just before the *Silver Swan* blew up . . .'

The fox looked as if he might be getting close to the chicken-run.

I started the tape again. There was a click. The background acoustic was quite different now. We were in Crispin Wharf House.

'Julian—what happened at King's Martlet last Saturday?'

The sound of my own voice made me jump. Darius gave my arm a squeeze.

Then came Julian's voice.

'Nothing happened at King's Martlet. The show was at Bettesham Court . . .'

I let the tape run on. I was getting a bit sleepy again, but

I noticed that the two men sat up when Philippa's voice was heard.

'It's quite true, Julian . . . the Contessa . . . Chris the candle-maker . . . Gussie Greenfingers . . . Charlie Spink . . . Verena Gadsden' (Darius drew in his breath sharply at that name), 'I've got plenty of cannabis from the last delivery . . . it's a universal currency . . .'

They listened intently to the rest of the conversation, right down to the moment when Julian said, 'I might as well have been speaking to a sack of potatoes.'

The fox glanced at Darius, and cleared his throat.

Philippa's voice was heard again for the last time.

'Goodbye, Julian. I'll go it alone . . .'

Then there was the appalling noise as the *Silver Swan* exploded. Flames roaring. Glass splintering. A terrible cry from Julian.

'The blast threw me against the desk and knocked me out for a bit,' I said. 'I don't expect the recorder picked up anything after that . . .'

But it did.

After a few minutes of odd shuffling sounds, the background acoustic changed again. We were out of doors.

'I ran down Magpie Lane,' I said. 'I wanted to get to the Magpie Inn and call the Fire Brigade . . .'

'They were already on their way,' said Darius.

There was a tremendous crash on the tape.

'That must be when I dropped the recorder,' I said. 'Well, I'm afraid that really is the end.'

The fox began talking to Darius. I went to switch off the recorder, but then I noticed that the spools were still turning. There was a lot of indistinct sound, then I could hear Mary as she rolled down the steps, getting closer and closer to the place where I had dropped the recorder. Then there was a cry as the iron bar fell across her.

'Wait a minute,' I said. 'There may be some more . . .'

The two men fell silent.

Then we heard my voice on the tape.

'A poison ring . . .'

And Mary's voice.

'I used it on Bunty Beresford . . . I had to get rid of her . . . *I* set up the cannabis operation . . . it started with Bamba . . . Verena and I went for a walk in the garden and I killed her with my ring . . .'

The grey fox was watching the spools revolve behind the small plastic window. Darius was holding me very tightly. And still the recording went on. At last there was a long silence, then distant sirens and hooting. Then a man's voice calling, 'Astolat! Darling, darling Astolat!'

The grey fox twinkled and switched off the recorder. Pity. That was the best bit of the whole tape.

I glanced up at Darius. His face seemed redder than I remembered. It didn't matter. He was still holding me close. I rested my head on his shoulder while he and the grey fox talked about unimportant matters.

They were looking at the photograph of Mr Um and the Rabbit at the St Valentine's Day party. How had they got hold of that? I remembered hazily that I'd left the wallet of photographs on the landing-stage when Darius gave me the cannabis-scented handkerchief and I ran home.

'The Customs men caught them,' I said. 'I saw them on television—they were with Charlie Spink at the airport. I don't know their real names.'

'*I* do,' said the fox, and he smiled, as though he'd be having Rabbit for supper.

'We'll pull in Madame Bamba and her friends,' he said. 'And the Contessa della whatnot . . .'

His voice became more and more distant.

I think I fell asleep.

I awoke to a smell of coffee and burning toast, and the sound of a knife rasping away the burnt bits. I discovered that I was curled up on the studio couch in my own flat.

Darius came in with a breakfast tray for two and I suddenly realized how very hungry I was.

He watched me in silence for a while, and then said, 'When did you last eat, Astolat?'

I considered the question, a piece of toast half way to my mouth.

'I had breakfast Saturday morning,' I said. 'I don't think I've had anything since then. What time is it now?'

'It's six o'clock on Sunday morning,' said Darius. 'I'll make some more toast . . .'

He went back to the kitchen, and while he was making the toast I sat up and found that I had been lying on a large crumpled-up ball of handkerchief. That was something that required an explanation. When Darius returned with the toast, I held the handkerchief out to him.

'When you gave me this handkerchief on the landing-stage on Friday night, did you know that it smelt of cannabis?'

'Of course I did,' he said. 'I wanted to see if you would recognize it. When you ran away, I hoped it was because I'd warned you to keep away from drug-traffickers and you'd taken the hint. You said you were going to the Motor Museum at Beaulieu, and I thought you were safely out of the way. Why the devil did you go back to Crispin Wharf House and fool about with Julian and his tape-recorder?'

As usual, when I needed words desperately, they wouldn't come. Because I love you. I couldn't say that.

Instead I said at last, 'Who are you, Darius, and whose side are you on?'

'I'm Darius Underwood, and I'm on the side of the angels.'

'Undercover drugs investigation?'

'M'mmm.'

'Is that why you went to Marrakech and all those other places?'

'Yes.'

'I read your *Marrakech Notebook*.'

There was an awkward pause.

'Look, Astolat, I've got a confession to make,' he said. 'I don't know how terrible this will seem to you, with all the books that you've written, but—well, I didn't write *Marrakech Notebook*—or any of the others.'

'You didn't?' I cried. 'But your photograph's on the cover . . .'

'Oh, the photograph's genuine,' he said. 'I was in Marrakech all right, but—well, when the old fox wanted me to infiltrate the Crispin Speakers' Agency he decided that my cover should be as a writer of travel books—he knew that I could give talks about the places all right. One of his friends introduced me to Mary as a potential recruit for the Agency. Mary thought she discovered me all by herself, but in fact I was foisted upon her . . .'

I gritted my teeth. He'd left out the really important thing.

'Darius—*who wrote those books?*'

'Oh—it was—a member of the department,' he said uneasily. 'Someone who'd been to all those places when he was a young man, and had still got the notebooks he'd written then. He'd always wanted to have them printed, and he didn't mind them going out under my name, so—'

'It was the fox!' I cried. 'The fox wrote them!'

I started to laugh, but Darius look at me very solemnly.

'Look, Astolat, I know you won't approve of my taking the credit for them—'

'Credit?' I gasped. '*Credit?* Darius, that Marrakech book is *terrible*. You can't think how relieved I am!'

'You're a funny girl,' he said. 'I thought you'd be furious because I hadn't written it.'

'No,' I said. 'I'd only have been furious with you if you *had* written it . . . So what was your job in Marrakech?'

'The same as it is anywhere, which is to keep my eyes and ears open,' he said. 'When I think the time is ripe, I pass the word along, the villains are rounded up and, we hope, put away for a long time.'

'But surely Crispin Speakers' Agency was just a—well, just a cottage industry. Weren't they rather small fish for you?'

'Small fish have a habit of attracting the attention of larger fish. There was a very big fish in the offing, and we regarded the Agency as bait. Well, we've lost the big fish for the moment. But don't forget, the Agency wasn't just into cannabis. They'd already moved on to the hard stuff. I didn't get a chance to find out how much there was in Crispin Wharf House, but Philippa certainly had half a kilo of cocaine stashed away in the *Silver Swan*, and at today's prices that's worth nearly a hundred thousand pounds.'

'Quite a lot of money for a cottage industry,' I murmured.

He nodded.

'And although Charlie Spink's pensioners were bringing in cannabis, Charlie himself was carrying cocaine in that walking-stick of his.'

'I suppose Charlie Spink upset everything,' I said.

'He certainly did. I knew Philippa was going to make a run for it when she asked me to get the *Silver Swan* ready for a long trip. She wouldn't have got far—we were waiting downstream for her—we wanted to catch her with the cocaine in her possession. But we never thought of Mary blowing the whole thing sky-high.'

'How did she do it?' I asked.

'Some simple device that went off when Philippa switched on the ignition, though I don't know where Mary picked up the electrical know-how to fix it.'

'In the theatre,' I said. 'She learned about stage lighting from her father—Bunty told me that. She must have been a competent electrician. And didn't you tell me that she knew how to handle the boat?'

He nodded.

'We never thought of Mary as the brains behind the

organization,' he said. 'We thought that she and Julian were being used as a cover. It was Philippa we were after . . .'

'Poor Philippa,' I said. 'I owe her a lot, Darius. You see, when I first met her I was hopelessly unsure of myself, but Philippa showed me that if only I wore romantic clothes I could go out into the world and fool people into thinking I was quite brave.'

I poured myself another cup of coffee, and was drinking it when it dawned on me that Darius was looking at me quizzically.

'I suppose you were wearing romantic clothes when you walked into Crispin Wharf House last night?' he said.

'Oh no,' I said. 'I couldn't have been. I was wearing—what I'm wearing now . . .'

'And you aren't under the impression that a T-shirt and jeans are at all romantic?'

'No,' I said slowly, and thought about it as I drank my coffee. I put the cup down unsteadily. 'Does that mean—do you think that means—?'

Darius leaned across the table and rested his hand on mine.

'I think, dear Astolat, it means that you are brave whatever clothes you are wearing.'

Once more I couldn't find any words, but the way that Darius was looking at me made me feel that perhaps words weren't all that necessary.

I don't know how long we sat there, me on the studio couch and Darius on the kitchen chair, looking at each other across the table with the cooling coffee and the crumbs of blackened toast.

At length the silence was broken by the sound of a distant church clock striking.

I said shakily, 'Philippa thought that romance was Celia Johnson saying goodbye to Trevor Howard on a railway station. I wonder—do you think—I mean—*I* think perhaps romance is sharing breakfast with you.'

M'mm,' said Darius. He shifted slightly in his chair. 'Only one thing wrong with it . . .'

'What's that?' I said. I couldn't see anything wrong with it at all.

'This chair I'm sitting on,' he said. 'It's terribly hard . . .'

He gave me one of his lovely, lazy smiles, and then he looked thoughtfully at my studio couch.

G